THE LAST MUSTER

LEONIE NORRINGTON

LIMINAL
BOOKS

This edition November 2020

ISBN 978-1-913544-16-4 (paperback)
ISBN 978-1-913544-17-1 (ebook)

Liminal Books

Dedicated to the memory of my brother Tony Izod.
For his children, Joanna, Jessica, Sam and James.

1

___

They're up past the jump-up, near Rochter's Pass, Shane and Red. It's morning time, late dry season. Around them tall pillars of stone reach into the sky, making the shadows dark and red. The ground is littered with shards of rock.

'I'm goin' around the other side,' Red says, standing up, stretching to get the bend out of her back. Her hat falls off behind her, leaving her red hair stuck flat against her forehead.

'Good hairdo!' Shane laughs.

'Shuddup,' she says, grabbing her hat and slamming it back on her head. 'You're myall.' She stomps away, disappearing behind a wall of stone.

They're looking for stone spearheads. Shane's great-grandfather started collecting weapons when he first came up here. Shane's got them lined up on a shelf in his bedroom: woomeras, ironwood killing spears, steel spearheads made from iron traded with the Macassans, white porcelain ones made out of insulators from the first Overland Telegraph line. They've got all that stuff from the early settlement period. The collection's finished, Shane reckons. But Red wants to find stone spearheads, ancient ones – perfect and deadly sharp. The ones her ancestors made before the malngarri, the white people, came.

Shane is crouching, his long legs up round his ears. He's fourteen, but already he's as tall as a man. There's something. . . What is it? Copper? He prises a small crumpled piece of metal out from between two rocks with his pocketknife. A bullet shell? He holds it up. Old one. Winchester .44. That's what the cops used in the old days. Lever action. *Peacemaker*, they called it.

The world's quiet, the stone walls hold in the silence.

Suddenly there's a tinkle of rock behind him.

Shane spins around, expecting to catch Red sneaking up on him to give him a fright.

But it's a horse. A huge chestnut stallion with a big roman nose. Must be a metre across the chest. No brumby, that's for sure. Gotta be a Quarter Horse or something. *Stay still. Don't scare him.*

'Hey big bloke. Where you come from?'

The stallion cocks his head, listening, brown eyes wide, skin trembling.

'Stand up,' Shane says. He's still got sugar in his pocket from this morning, from when he was training his horse Chocolate. 'You right,' he says, getting a cube of sugar out and offering it, palm up, to the horse.

The sweetness fills the air.

The stallion's nostrils twitch and flare.

'That's it,' Shane says, stepping forward.

The stallion recognises the sweet smell. He jerks his head up, knocking the sugar into the air, and dives at Shane, teeth bared.

Shane jumps back, trips, rolls and takes off. The horse is right behind him, front legs lashing out, mouth open, eyes white. Shane scrambles up the rock face to a ledge, safe.

The stallion rears, singing out, pawing the air. A group of mares behind him watch, their ears pricked forward, alert. He wheels round, forces the mares into a tight group, and with his head down, threatening to bite them, he hunts them down the slope.

Shane watches, stunned.

'What's-a matter?' Red comes flying around the corner, holding her hat on with her hand. 'Shane!'

'Nothing.'

'Don't gammon.' Red yells, hands on hips, legs apart. Little dark freckles stand out across her nose. 'Where are you?'

Shane's on a ledge, a small cave in the rock face. He can see Red, but she can't see him. Deadly. He opens his hand; the copper bullet shell sits in his palm. There's a little recess in one of the walls. A pile of . . . bullet heads? He picks them up. They're definitely bullet heads, covered with years of dust. They're whole. Still perfect. Not dented or scratched with the impact of hitting something hard. They've been shot into something soft. They've been dug out of . . . a body? He holds one of the bullets against the shell. It's the same.

'Shane! Stop stuffing around!' Red's voice is urgent.

He puts the bullet heads and the shell in his pocket and stands up. 'It was just a brumby,' he says, climbing down. 'Took off down there.' He jumps the last metre to the ground and runs to the edge of the hill to watch the horses go down the slope. But . . .

'They're gone!'

'Where?' Red walks over, shaking her head, thinking, *As if.*

'No bull, Red,' he says. 'Dead set! Look! It was a stallion.' He shows her the broken twigs, the stomped grass, the hoof tracks in the soil between the rocks.

'He hunted you.' Red reads the hoof-prints aloud.

Shane says nothing, shame prickling the skin on his face.

'Foal,' Red says, pointing to a tiny hoof-print.

'Where?' Shane comes over to see for himself. 'They can't have foals this time of year.'

There's no grass anywhere. Without food the mare's milk will dry up and the foal will starve.

Red and Shane follow the horses' tracks down the slope. Here a flattened clump of grass, there a clear hoof-print in the bare earth. Then, suddenly, there's nothing.

They look at each other and back at the ground, searching, searching.

But there's nothing. Absolutely nothing.

They stop and listen for movement. Not a sound.

They are two dots on the edge of a hillside. Around them the redness of the Kimberley stretches out for hundreds of kilometres. Rocks and spinifex, cliffs, gorges and caves. In the flat country below them they can just make out their home, Turkey Flat station. The tin roofs of the generator shed, the big house and the workshop shine in the sunlight.

'Must be Roman,' Dad says later. He and Shane are in the bull-catcher coming back from the bore run – a 200-kilometre round trip to fill the tanks and troughs for the cattle in the dry country.

'Who?'

'Roman. Killiara station Quarter Horse. Mad as a cut snake. Bolted from the Opium Springs camp draft 'bout ten year ago. Took every mare in the camp. Million bucks in horseflesh gone in one night.'

'Roman nose? Chestnut?'

'That's him,' Dad says. 'Going to have to shoot the bugger or he'll bolt with all our mares.' He shakes his head, reaching into his pocket for his tobacco. He's steering with his knee while he rolls a smoke, his fingers thick, the skin like dark leather against the fragile rice-paper.

'Couldn't we trap him, Dad?'

'Nah. You'd never get him. Too cunning. When he first took off, they tried everything to get that horse back. Even sent a chopper in, sneaking into the holes, trying to sniff him out. Never set eyes on any of 'em. Twenty-odd horses disappeared into thin air.'

'Has no one seen them since?'

'People reckon they seen tracks. But never in the flesh.'

Shane smiles. *Deadly.*

In the distance, boab trees stand like massive bottles in the yellow dust. There's been no rain for six months and the ground is almost bare, even the dry grass is gone.

'Why ya up Rochter's Pass anyway?'

'Just looking for spearheads and stuff.'

'Watch yourself up there, mate. Easy to get bushed in them rocks.'

'I know it pretty good now.'

'You can't know that country, son,' Dad says, licking the paper and rolling it into a neat tube. 'Don't take it for granted is all I'm saying.'

'Lofty knows that country.'

'Yeah. But he's Bunuba – that's different. He knows what's going on.'

They drive along in silence.

'A murderer hid up there for years one time,' Dad says. 'Bunuba bloke. They had half the police force in Australia looking for him. Never found him.'

'A murderer?' Shane feels the bullet heads in his pocket.

'When they were first opening up this country, the Bunuba killed cattle, hid up in the stone country, ambushed ringers, police patrols. They killed a couple of malngarri – bastards probably deserved it if the truth be known – they were pretty tough on the Bunuba in them days.'

'What was his name?'

'I don't know.' Dad shrugs his shoulders, thinking. 'Pigeon, I think. Something like that.'

'They get him?'

'Nah. Gave up trying to settle this country for years. Your great-grandad reckons when he first came here as a young bloke, he was too scared to sleep at night. He used to take catnaps during the day under a tree or on horseback. Never slept in the same place twice in case he got speared.'

'Big stallion up there today,' Red tells her grandad Old Lofty in Language, pointing up to the stone country with her lips.

He looks at her and lifts his eyebrows asking, *Where?*

'Past the jump-up near Julugjuluyin,' she continues in Language. 'Big chestnut horse. Huge one, Shane reckons. With a roman nose. I didn't see it myself.'

Lofty looks up at Balili, the stone country. He's sitting on an upturned kero tin near his cooking fire. The camp-oven murmurs in the coals and the smell of roast beef fills the air.

Lofty's a tall man, skinny. His skin closes tight over the bones on his face, thousands of tiny points of white hair roughen his dark chin, curly white hair stands up around his face. Lofty was born on the station. He worked as Shane's great-grandfather's 'boy' and then out in the stock camps. He grew into a tall, strong man, a good ringer. But every wet season his mother's brother took him back bush, to do his ceremonies, to learn the country – the songs and stories of the land. So he learned two ways. One side the ceremony man, the other side head stockman. For more than fifty years he was boss for all the Turkey Flat stock camps, including the outstations.

Now he's meant to be retired. But he still lives at the station in the same little tin donga he built for himself in the 1950s. It's down by the cattle yards, rusted purple and orange with age, blackened with smoke from cooking fires and sinking into the earth with memories and time. Most of the Bunuba people got hunted off the country when the Company took over the station, but Lofty stayed – they couldn't move him. Or Red, he didn't let her go either.

2

———

That night Shane wanders down from the big house to sit with Red and Lofty by the fire. The stars hang bright in the sky. The air is cold. They pull their jackets and blankets around them, and hold pannikins of hot tea with both hands for warmth.

'Lofty, you subbie that murderer name Pigeon?' Shane asks, in Kriol. 'Dad reckon, olden time, there was one Bunuba man name Pigeon killing station people, spearing cattle round here.'

Lofty shrugs his shoulders.

Red looks at her grandfather. That's Jandamarra Shane's talking about. Malngarri call him Pigeon. Grandad knows that. He's always telling her stories about Jandamarra. How he fought the settlers that were trying to steal his country for their cattle. How he could run forty miles in a day without showing his tracks. How he killed that policeman, took all his guns, and hid in the hills to ambush the invaders and kill their cattle.

Silence.

Shane realises Lofty doesn't want to talk about it and changes the subject. 'What about that stallion? Red tell you? Dad reckon mightbe that Quarter Horse now, from Killiara station.'

Lofty nods. 'Mightbe.'

'Dad's gonna shoot him. Reckons he'll float with all our mares.'

Lofty cocks his head to listen, lifting his finger for silence.

They look at him, questioning.

'That's that horse now.' He points with his lips to the floodplain. 'Listen him?'

Shane and Red shake their heads.

'There,' the old man says, and makes the sound himself so they know what to listen for. 'You got him?'

'Yeah.' Red catches the sound.

'Gammon,' Shane says, annoyed.

'There!' Red says, and Shane does hear something. A snort? A horse clearing its nose of dust? A body shaking to chase the mozzies away? Yes, there's something there alright.

Red and Shane smile at each other. The foal will be right if its mother can feed on the floodplain.

They sit listening. The air fills with swift movements and whispering whistles as tiny bats dart around the camp, catching insects.

'We should get them horses,' Shane says. 'Make a donkey trap. Put a mineral block inside. We might catch the whole lot. Get one mare for you Red.'

'More better you leave them be,' Lofty says, his voice stern.

Silence.

Shane and Red look at each other. What's wrong with Lofty? Normally he'd be really excited about catching something wild. What about the time they trapped a mob of clean-skins? He even helped them build the trap then. What's so different this time?

Lofty gets up and goes inside to get more tobacco.

'Red,' Shane whispers. 'We got a day off school tomorrow.'

Red and Shane do Correspondence. It's their first year of high school. They've got a proper teacher, Miss Mandy, who talks to them over the radio. But Shane's mum works with them every day. 'The teacher from hell' she calls herself, laughing, but it's not funny. She is! She goes on and on. Arguing, trying to make Shane write things when there's nothing in his head.

Red loves school. She loves making neat rows of writing and coloured borders and title pages. 'If you spent as much time writing as you did on the title page, Red, you'd get an A every time,' Shane's mum says. But whenever Red takes her work down to Lofty, he thinks she's the smartest girl in the world. She loves reading out her essays and projects to him and seeing his face, real proud.

Shane hates school; the radio, the endless pages – white, empty, waiting to be filled with fear and humiliation. The best thing about doing Correspondence, he reckons, is that they get to take days off to help with the station work. Like tomorrow, they've got the day off school to help muster the cattle.

'Let's stay home in the morning and make a trap for the horses,' Shane says. 'We can take the old ute up.'

'And miss out on the muster?'

'They're doing Goose Creek and Dry River first. They won't get back here till afternoon time. We can make the trap in the morning and be back dinnertime to help with the cattle.'

Red screws up her face, not sure if it's a good idea.

'Imagine having one of them Quarter Horse mares, Red,' Shane says, leaning forward. 'I could teach you how to train her. You could really show all that town mob.'

'You don't need to tell me how to train a horse!' Red sneers, but her heart beats faster, thinking about a horse of her own. She always has to ride the stock-horses. Sometimes Shane lets her ride his horse Chocolate at a gymkhana or rodeo. And Chocolate's good and smart and quick. But if she had her own horse – a horse that she could break in herself and teach – it would be ...

a powerful Quarter Horse mare, intelligent and beautiful. A chestnut. No! A bay, with a long black mane. And I would plait ribbons and beads into her tail like the native Americans. And put a handprint in white ochre on her rump. Comanche! I'd call her Comanche and we'd take out everything at the rodeos and gymkhanas: the barrel race, the breakaway roping, the steer un-decorating. 'And here's Red from Turkey Flat station, heading for the finals,' the bloke on the loudspeaker sings out. And I'd just look around at them mob and smile. All them whispering girls. Show them good and proper.

'We'll gammon stay home to do schoolwork – that essay – independent one,' Shane says.

'What?' Red's still caught in her fantasy.

'We'll tell them we're gonna finish that essay and we'll stay here and build the trap for the horses.'

Red looks dubious.

'Come on. Miss Mandy will back us up if Mum doesn't believe us. She told us we should get it done first thing,'

Shane says. 'If we can get that essay finished in the morning, we'll have the rest of term free of English.'

Red nods.

Old Lofty comes back and they quickly change the subject.

A whistle pierces the still air. Dad's calling the dogs in for their feed.

'See you mob,' Shane says, getting up to go. He whistles softly, calling the dogs as he walks up to the big house, teasing them. They run toward him and run back. They want to jump all over him but want to stay near Dad to get their food.

'Leave them be,' Dad says, gammon grumpy.

Shane collects the dishes up off the ground and Dad fills them.

The rattle of dried dog food and the chunks of frozen meat hitting the tin dishes makes the dogs' mouths drool. They sit down, stand up, spin around in quick circles and sit down again. Their eyes glisten with expectation. They look Dad straight in the eye as he puts their food in front of them, waiting for him to say 'Right-oh' so they can scoff it down.

Away from the veranda lights, the night is dark. The stars hang so close that Dad and Shane look up, caught for a moment by the expanse of the Milky Way spread out across the sky.

'Got an early start in the morning. Choppers will be here at six,' Dad says, walking back inside.

'How come we're mustering again so soon?'

'Greed, mate,' Dad says. 'Corporate bloody greed. Two thousand head they want.' His voice is bitter with disgust. 'We're already flogging the guts out of the country and they want more.'

. . .

Shane's in bed, the bullet heads heavy in his palm. *What about that ledge, hey? I was only three metres away and Red couldn't see me. And Pigeon? Lofty knows about him. Of course he does. He knows everything. Why didn't he want to talk about it? Is Pigeon still up there? Nah, he'd be a hundred years old by now. But I bet he was on that ledge. I bet they shot him and he dug these bullets out of his own body.*

The generator slows and dies. The outside lights falter and go out. Darkness. Silence. Then the night sounds fill the space and Shane tries to hear the horses on the floodplain. Nothing. He thinks about that stallion. *Ever seen anything so perfect? Like one of those million-dollar cutting horses in* Hoofs and Horns. *Imagine owning him. Training him. Getting him working – a one-man horse. Have to break him in slow – respectful. Make him want to learn, eager to please like Chocolate – she's good and smart but too small.* He puts his hands behind his head and stretches his legs out in front of him. *Yep. Need a man's horse now.*

Red and Lofty hear the generator die. Their fire flickers. An orange glow spreads out in a circle into the darkness. With the lights from the big house gone, the night settles in closer around them.

'Grandad?' Red says in Language.

Lofty looks at her. He knows that tone. She wants something.

'I want my own horse.'

'Leave it,' Lofty says in Language. 'Leave that horse be. There's plenty of horses around here for you to ride.'

'But I want a good horse. A smart horse,' Red says. 'I want a horse I can train. Not a myall old brumby! I want to prove ...' tears catch in her voice. She gets up and storms away to bed and wraps her blanket tight around her.

The darkness creeps over Lofty, making him shiver. *What's happening? Another muster already? And that horse. What's he doing here? He normally stays over Gulinyin way. And Shane asking questions about Jandamarra? Red desperate and angry? Prove what, young girl? There's too many things happening in this one day. Coincidence? Nah. Something's up — some big change is coming.* He pulls his blanket up around his shoulders and slumps down into his chair, closing in on himself, his body blending into the darkness as the firelight dies.

3

———

Long before dawn the big house is bustling. The whistle of the kettle boiling, sausages, tomatoes and eggs frying in the pan, boots clumping on the wooden floorboards; guns, bullets, stock-whip, Esky, water bottles beside the door. Directions and expectations for the day hang in the air between mouthfuls of breakfast and slurps of tea.

Red stays in bed. She doesn't trust herself to get up and face Grandad. She won't be able to hide her excitement and he'll know she's up to something.

'Red!' he calls, just before dawn.

'Staying here,' she answers. 'Got homework to do.'

He stands looking at her in disbelief. *Miss out on a muster? What the hell's wrong with you?* But she keeps her eyes closed, hiding from the questions she can feel on her skin.

Lofty says nothing. He makes a billy, wraps the leftover roast in a flour-bag and sits on his kero tin, sipping his tea and waiting.

· · ·

The chopper arrives at first light, its motor screaming, blowing dust and leaf litter into the air.

'Must have left before he could see,' Dad says with reverence. He grabs his dinner Esky and, holding his hat, runs hunched over beneath the blades and climbs in. They take off, tipping forward and slipping across the open land, out and up into the sky.

Mum rinses the dishes, wipes the benches, loads the car. 'Give us a hand, Shane.'

She jumps in the Toyota. 'Come on,' she says to him. 'What you doing? Jump in.'

'Nah, not going, got that essay to finish. It's due next week. I'll come and help once you get back here.'

'It's right,' she says, feeling sorry for him. 'We'll do it later. Come on. Everyone's going to be there for Goose Creek and Dry River.'

'But I've got it all worked out now,' Shane says, trying to make his voice sound sincere. 'May as well finish it. Then it's done.'

Mum holds his gaze.

Shane looks at the air between them, keeping his face deadly serious. His guts are churning with the lie.

'Red's coming.'

'Nah, she's going to stay here too. We're gonna work on it together.'

Mum looks at him for a moment longer, trying to see what's going on in his head. Something's up: she knows it. *Give him the benefit of the doubt,* she thinks. *He might be doing the essay, you don't know.* Anyway, she doesn't want to think about it. Today she's out of the house. Away from the schoolwork, the kitchen, the walls. Away from trying to get the kids enthusiastic about stuff she hates herself. She'll be outside, in the bush. The dust in the morning air, the smell of cattle, damper in the fire at dinnertime. *And there's a breakaway. She sees herself flying along, the power of the motor under her feet, spinning the steering wheel, the Toyota swerving around trees and rocks. The wheels skidding in the dirt, her heart thumping loud with excitement as she turns the bullock back to the herd.*

She takes off down to Lofty's place. He's sitting on his kero tin dressed, boots, hat, long-sleeved shirt. He smiles at her to say, *We're going mustering.* Mum smiles back to say, *You're not wrong!*

Shane stands in the doorway, watching them leave, trying to look dejected as he waves, as if he's going to spend the whole day doing schoolwork.

Red jumps out of bed, pulls on her clothes, hat, boots. Sneaks her head out behind the wall to check they've really gone and runs up to the big house, her head light with excitement. Shane meets her at the gate.

'Let's take the ute.' He's already running toward the machinery shed.

'Not the ute – can't get high enough. The quad bike! We'll get further on the quad bike.'

'The trail bike,' they both say as they run into the shed.

In this country, at the base of the hills, the land dips into basins – little valleys. If Shane and Red had been on foot or on horseback they would have looked ahead. Knowing the curve of the hills, they wouldn't have bothered investigating. But they're on the trail bike, and Shane's concentrating on the ground right in front of him. They're following wallaby tracks to make it easier, dodging around rocks, lifting their legs out of spiky clumps of spinifex. So they don't notice that they're climbing higher and higher along the slope. Don't notice that they're going back into the hill they've just passed, until suddenly there's a gap in front of them – a slit like a knife-cut in a wall of rock, blue sky shining through.

They stop, too stunned to speak.

Shane turns the bike off.

They step off, stand the bike up and walk the few steps to the gap. The rock's cool, sheltered from the sun by the tall cliffs. Its redness is covered with pale cream lichen and dark dribblings where water has trickled over it for thousands of years.

As they go out of the hot sun, Red's skin lifts into goose-bumps. It's like air-conditioning oozing from the rocks. She leans against the wall for a moment. Then, together, she and Shane step through the gap.

Into a huge valley.

Like a crater surrounded by sheer cliffs, one hundred metres high, the stone glowing red in the sunlight.

'This must be where they went, the horses,' Shane says, looking down at the ground.

But there aren't any horse hoof-prints on the sandy path. There's kangaroo tracks, their large softness tipped with sharp points; there's curlew tracks, neat deliberate steps one directly in front of the other; there's tracks of bandicoots and rock wallabies, but no horses.

This is where Jandamarra hid, Red thinks. *One of his secret valleys, where he hid when the police were hunting him. Where he put that mob of cattle so no one could find them. I don't think we should come here without permission.*

The vegetation is dense. It hasn't been burnt for years. The canopy so thick, there's no grass underneath it. The ground is covered with a layer of leaves. And over there, on the left-hand side, there's a line of dark green vegetation defining a spring-fed creek.

Suddenly Shane's thirsty, really thirsty. They left the water bottle back on the bike. He imagines sitting in a deep pool of clear water, tree roots matted into dark walls. There's a clear path between the trees. He starts walking along the path, down from the rocky hillside into the valley, heading for the creek.

'Shane!' Red calls out. She's thirsty too, but she doesn't trust this place. Something's wrong.

'Heaps of bush tucker!' Shane says. 'This place is excellent. We could live here.'

The path's wide and clear, regularly used, heading straight down the slope into the thick forest. Amazing. Even at this driest time of the year, there's fungi on the dead wood.

'Look,' Shane says, walking off the path. 'Check this out, Red.' He points to a huge bright orange fungus, pure white on the edges.

'Don't touch it!' Red yells.

'Just having a look.' He walks back through the bush to meet the path further down. The land drops quickly away and he can see right into the valley.

'Wow! Red! Look!'

Green. An open expanse of green grass. Bright wet season green. Impossible. Must be the light. There's no green grass anywhere at this time of year.

They run back to the path to get a better view – to see if

it's true. And there it is, spread out before them, a huge flat of thick bright green grass. *Barurra*, Red thinks.

'Deadly' Shane starts toward it.

'Shane!' Red shakes her head, telling him not to go any further.

Why? he asks with his eyes.

She shudders. Something is wrong. But what? The creek water sparkles, but there are no waterbirds. There's no wallabies, no cattle, no horses, not even birds flying above. No movement, no noise. 'I'm going back,' she says. 'I'm thirsty.'

'Let's get a drink at the creek,' Shane says.

Red shakes her head, turns, and starts walking back. A hawk calls out loud and clear.

Shane looks up into the sky. Nothing.

It calls again, closer. And there it is. In the tree just above him, watching.

'It's a crested hawk, Red,' Shane yells.

The crested hawk looks down at him, yellow eyes still and focused. Crested hawks don't live in this country. They live in the thicker forests along the big rivers.

Red's gone.

Turning back, he scans this new world, the green flat, the forest of bush tucker trees and, all around, the sheer cliffs of red stone – it's like a sunken paradise. *Can't wait to show Dad. Bet he never knew this was here.* And he runs up the path to find Red.

4

Red is almost running when he catches up with her.

'Red, wait! What's the hurry? This place is perfect for the trap.'

She keeps walking, fast.

'We'll put that salt lick down on the floodplain,' Shane says, following her. 'Give the horses a taste for it.'

She doesn't answer, stepping over rocks and tree roots. The path seems smaller, less used.

'Red, you listening? Once they get a taste for it, we can lure them in here. Build the donkey trap in the gap. We'll catch them, no worries.'

Red suddenly stops and Shane bumps into her. 'Whatcha doing?'

'It's gone.'

'What?' Shane pushes around her.

The gap's gone! There's a sheer cliff of stone smack in front of them!

'It can't be.' Shane pushes the rock, not believing his eyes. It's solid.

He spins around, looking at the ground.

We must have taken the wrong path.

But there was only one path.

This is the one we came in on, definitely. We came through the gap and walked down through those trees. Down and back. We didn't turn off.

Shane turns back to the stone wall. Takes a deep breath. *Think clearly.* 'This isn't the track we came in on,' he says slowly, following the track with his hand as it heads straight for the wall, then narrows and goes into a burrow under the rock. 'It's all right. We just took the wrong track.'

Red doesn't move.

Shane looks down at the ground again. 'Look. No footprints. Our footprints aren't there. We didn't come in this way. We must be on the wrong track.'

Red squats down to look.

There are no human footprints on the ground at all.

None coming in. None coming back up the path to where they're standing.

She looks up at Shane, a big hole opening up in her chest.

Think! Think! Shane's mind screams. *There's got to be an explanation.*

He puts his foot down on the sandy path, lifts it up again and looks beneath. The soft sand falls back into place. No footprint.

'We're not here,' Red says.

'It's all right,' Shane says out loud. 'We'll just head back down and find the right track. Come on.' He reaches out to grab Red's hand and they start walking.

The track's only one person wide, barely visible. They have to push back overhanging branches and skirt big rocks, focusing on the ground all the time so they don't trip.

And then there's a noise.

Not really a noise – more like a thudding in the air.

Their footfalls?

They stop.

No, it's still there.

The noise is so quiet at first, like a heartbeat among the crickets and the rustles of leaves.

But it gets louder. What is it?

They move close together.

It gets louder and louder until the noise fills the air, bouncing off the rock walls, slamming against their chests and ringing in their ears. Where's it coming from? There's nothing in the sky. It's not coming from the trees.

Then it's gone.

Silence. A silence which leaves a vacuum so deep they have to listen hard to hear the soft sounds of insects in the trees.

Don't panic. Panic is what gets people killed. Shane hears his father's voice. *If you're in a car, stay with it. Someone will find you. If you have to move, think clearly before you do and stay on the track!* His body is suddenly weak, heavy, pressing him down to the ground, his guts empty, his legs jittering so much he has to crouch down and gammon check the ground for footprints before he falls.

Red leans her leg against Shane's arm. She pulls herself up tall and, looking out at the country, says softly in Language, 'I am Redeleenia. Granddaughter for that old man Lofty, working station long time. Head stockman. Law man. Countryman.'

Shane leans into her leg.

'I'm Redeleenia,' Red says again, louder this time. 'Granddaughter for that old man Lofty, working station long time.

Head stockman. Law man. Countryman. I come here by mistake. I mean no offence.'

Silence. No birds. No bees on the flowers. Nothing.

Shane forces himself to stand beside her. They pull themselves up tall and look out into the valley, trying to look brave and strong.

Thirsty. Shane's really thirsty. 'Gotta get a drink. Where's the creek-line?'

They scan the valley. All the bush looks the same now. Taller if anything – it seems taller and thicker, but there's no line of green.

'It was there on the left. Over there.'

Red nods. 'Yes, it was right there,' she says, lifting her right arm.

'No! You're pointing right, Red. That's right.'

'It was there,' she says, pointing to the right-hand side of the valley.

'But I remember saying... It was left. I remember thinking it was on the left.'

They breathe slow and deliberate, sucking ordinary normal air into their lungs. Forcing their hearts to slow down to stop the adrenalin pumping through their veins, making their brains fuzzy.

'Thirsty. Need a drink bad,' Red says, the inside of her mouth tacky with dried saliva.

'If we can get down to that creek ... ' Shane tries to sound confident, and takes a couple of steps down the track. But there are tracks going everywhere. Big ones. Small ones. Tiny bare lines through the leaf litter where mice and rock rats scamper. Tunnels through the undergrowth where rock wallabies push their way through. Large pads going around rocks and trees worn totally bare by feet. By feet? But there are no footprints. Even the wallaby and the curlew prints are gone.

Red grabs Shane's arm. 'Stay up here. If there's a way out, a gap, it'll be up here in the cliffs.'

If! Shane thinks. *If* there's a way out? What do you mean *if?*

'Come on.' Red starts climbing up toward the big rocks that lie beneath the cliff face.

It's hot. Sweat dribbles down their faces, making little rivers, tickling their skin as it slides under their shirts, across their bellies. The sun's high in the sky. The heat hits the rock face and bounces back at them, blistering hot.

We're trapped, Shane's thinking. *There's no way out. And there's something funny about this place. What if it isn't really here, like in* The Lion, the Witch and the Wardrobe? *What if we've stepped into another world? Another dimension?*

High above them the crested hawk circles, floating on the warm air rising from the rock walls. It's watching the humans, as vulnerable as rock rats, following one another as they climb over and around boulders, exposed to the open sky, little dots of darkness against that great glare of rock.

Beneath the stone walls it's so quiet that at first, they only hear the noise on their skin. But then it's there again. Thumping, bouncing against their chests. Coming at them from all directions at once. Stinging their eardrums. Coming closer and closer. It's definitely coming from the sky. *And we're out in the open. Exposed like mice.*

'Run!' Red grabs Shane's hand and they run, jumping over rocks, ducking under vines, dodging trees; the noise right behind them, bouncing off fallen logs, thud-thudding against their backs. They can't go fast enough. Wait-a-bit vines grab at their clothes, cutting into their skin as they tear away. Still they run, down, down, into the forest, till the scrub's so thick they can't go any further; and they crouch against a tree trunk, their heartbeats thudding loud in their ears.

$$5$$

The noise is still there, but much quieter. It can't get through the dense vegetation. It stays above them, bouncing around the valley.

'What is it? What do you reckon it is?' Shane whispers.

Red shrugs her shoulders and looks down, playing with the leaves on the ground between her legs.

Is this the land before time? Shane thinks. *Was that gap in the rock wall a time warp that opened up for an instant and then closed again forever? Is this the land of dinosaurs? No, they don't make a noise like that. They screech. Wait a minute! Scientists don't know what sort of noise dinosaurs made. This place might have been cut off from the rest of the world for thousands, millions of years.*

Whatever it was, he thinks, *the way it was moving, it was definitely hunting.*

He gets up. 'I gotta have a look.'

'Don't!' Red grabs his arm. 'Sit quiet. Grandad and your Dad will come and find us.'

'But, no one knows this place, Red. It might not even be here.'

He starts to climb the tree.

'Shane.'

'I'll just go to the canopy. It won't see me.'

'But you don't know how it looks. What it uses for eyes,' Red yells after him, but he doesn't listen. She sits down, wrapping her arms around her knees. *This is so bad.*

Leave him, her thoughts say. *Just crawl. Just keep crawling downhill and you'll find a crystal-clear spring. Lie in it, let the water soak into you, suck the sparkling clear water into your body.*

She holds her knees tight. *Stay where you are,* she tells herself. *Don't listen. Grandad said spirits can get into your mind and lure you away. You gotta think of something else. Think of a song. What?* Her brain is empty. *Your favourite song. Yes. Got it.* 'Would the real Buffalo Bill please stand . . .' She sings the words out loud, rocking her body, filling her mind with the music to chase the thoughts of water away. ' . . . holding a beer and a gun in each hand.'

Shane climbs up the tree. The noise gets louder and louder, filling his ears until they're aching, making him dizzy. And then he sees it. A huge black dragonfly. Dark against the blue sky, it comes up behind the valley wall, turns its tail up into the air and dives straight down again.

The chopper! It's the mustering chopper! The familiar *chugga, chugga* noise is disguised as it bounces and echoes off the stone walls.

Why didn't I think of that? Relief floods through his body, making his arms and legs weak. Then he starts to laugh. *'What'd you think it was, you idiot? A dinosaur or something?'*

The chopper appears again – lifting up into the blueness above the cliff, hovering this time, getting a good vantage point to see any strays, then turning its tail up, dropping forwards and chasing them towards the yards.

Releasing his grip, Shane slides down the tree trunk. 'It's the chopper, Red,' he yells, jumping to the ground. 'It's just the noise from the mustering chopper bouncing off the walls.'

'No way!' Red stands up. 'We should sing out to them, get their attention. They could get us out of here.'

'There's nowhere to land.'

'That flat near the creek, quick!'

But the noise has gone.

They wait and hear nothing.

They're alone.

The forest talks around them, loud in the silence. Insects buzz, birds flit between the trees, native bees hum in the Horsfieldia flowers, tall timber creaks as it moves.

The light changes. *Sun must have gone behind a cloud. Dark, really dark. Is the scrub thicker?*

'Come on. Let's get out of here,' Shane says, turning around to go.

But which way? Huge tree trunks stick up like poles all around them. It looks the same in every direction.

Dark shadows lift and move. The air is still. The only sound is the little rustles in the leaves – *lizards?*

Or are the trees moving?

Red pulls herself up tall. *Don't see them. Don't let them talk to you. Just think about which way to go.*

'How come the chopper's here?' she asks, her voice soft. 'Grandad said the chopper wouldn't be back till after dinnertime.'

'Don't know. What time is it?'

She shrugs.

'I'll just have a look at the sun,' he says, climbing back up the tree.

With his arms wrapped around the trunk, standing on a high branch, Shane looks out. The sun's low in the sky. *What? It can't be that late!* But it is. A heavy shadow from the cliff on the western side has spread right across the valley.

A shimmer of panic spreads through his body. *What the hell is happening?*

'What time is it?' Red yells up.

'It's about three o'clock.'

'What!' she says, looking up the trunk.

'It's late. We're in big trouble.' Shane climbs down the tree.

'No way! The sun was high when we . . .'

'It's all right. It's good. Now we can work by the sun,' Shane says, trying to stay calm. *Don't think about it. It's okay.* 'The sun's setting over there, so that's west.' He grabs a stick and clears a space in the leaves, forgetting that the ground won't hold a mark. 'We came up the jump-up. That's due south of the homestead.' He makes marks in the dark crumbly soil. 'Here's the jump-up. We came this way. We must be about here.'

They both look at the lines in the soil. The soil holds the map. And beside it are handprints, footprints. Their footprints!

'The gap we came through should be that way. Up in that cliff.' Red tries to sound confident.

'We just took the wrong track,' Shane says.

They walk quickly through the tangle of scrub toward the cliff, then as soon as it's open enough they run. Too scared to slow down in case their luck changes, they run to the tumble of red rocks and the valley wall.

Which way?

'Keep the sun at your back,' Shane calls, scrambling over rocks around scrubby trees, heading for the great wall of stone.

Then they're on the path, their feet padding on the soft sand.

And the gap's right there.

They run straight for it. Not game to stall or look at the ground, not game to take their eyes off the gap for a second, in case it closes over again.

They're through!

The bike. Quick!

They push the bike down the hill, over rocks and spinifex. They jump on, slam it into gear, and race along the gravel slope to the road. Shane pulls back the throttle to full and they fly along, dust spinning out behind them, out through the open bushland, to the cleared ground where the bush becomes paddocks; predictable, where the country is settled, with fences and laneways, roads and drains. The dark shape of the stone country stands silent behind them.

6

'Not gonna get back in time,' Red screams over the roar of the bike.

The helicopter is already doing the first sweep, zigzagging across the land, hunting cattle through the open bushland. The cattle run in small groups, dust lifting up behind them. The chopper backs up and turns, heading back to clear the next area, gathering more cattle and worrying them into a large herd like a sheepdog, then hunting them down to where Mum and Lofty are waiting to push them into the spelling yard. There's no way Shane and Red can get back to the house without being seen.

Shane slows the bike down. 'What're we gonna do?'

'Chopper's probably seen us. Have to gammon we've come out to help,' Red says. 'If we can get back into the bush . . .'

They hear the chopper's siren, and see it hovering above a thick clump of trees, dipping in too close to the canopy, cutting back and diving in again. Must be a mob of cattle in there, too scared to move.

Excellent! Shane thinks. 'Hang on!' He pulls back on the throttle, making the front wheel lift off the ground.

Red laughs and grabs him round the waist to stop falling off.

And they're flying along so fast the trees are just ribbons of grey and brown at the edge of their vision.

There are the bullocks huddled together, their heads ducked, hiding from the siren. Shane and Red ride out of the trees, waving at the chopper to say, *We will get them out.*

Dad's arm comes out of the cockpit, thumbs up: *No worries! Thanks!*

Shane spins the back wheel, sending dirt and dust into the air. Dad shakes his head, *you're a ratbag*, as the chopper lifts up and away.

Shane and Red go around behind the cattle, deliberately slow. The cattle look up, recognise the bike and start to stir. But they stay in a group. Shane revs the bike louder, moving toward them, forcing them to break and run out of the trees. Then he's turns the bike from side to side, gathering them into a group. One baulks. Shane slows, whistles, gets around him, and pushes him gently back into the mob again.

When the cattle are clear of the trees, the chopper swoops in to take over, getting in behind them and pushing. Then it lifts higher, turning around and coming down on them quick, sending them rushing in a cloud of dust down to the temporary hessian-covered fence that will force them into the laneway.

Shane stops the bike and he and Red watch.

'You right!' Red says, slapping Shane's back. 'Scaring the hell out of me!'

'What? That wasn't fast!' He laughs, stretches his long legs down either side of the bike, gammon real tough.

'Rearing up like that. You coulda threw me.'

'Take more than that to throw you,' he laughs.

She pushes him in the back and smiles, proud.

They watch the helicopter diving at the cattle – too close.

'He's cocky that pilot. Why don't he just let them run?'

A bullock breaks from the herd and bolts.

'See what I mean?'

The chopper tips away to follow it and bring it back. The rest of the mob starts breaking apart.

'Hang on!' Shane yells, and they take off.

The bullock is galloping flat out, the chopper right behind it.

The bike screams as Shane flattens it, getting around the chopper so Dad can see him, waving his arms to say, *Leave it – the mob's breaking up.*

Dad yells at the chopper pilot and they head back to the main herd.

The bike and the bullock are parallel, about ten metres apart. Shane brings the bike in close, really close.

The bullock tries to put on more speed but the bike gets in front, cutting him off.

He turns.

They could just push him back to the herd but . . .

'Stay with him. Knock him up,' Red yells.

Shane nods. Red wants to throw him.

They stay right behind the bullock, making him go faster, faster. Blaring the horn, trying to knock him up. But he's strong, he keeps going and going, getting closer to the herd. Red's gonna miss her chance if he gets back with the mob.

Then just when Red's about to give up, he starts running in long loping jumps, exhausted.

'That's him. Get in close,' Red yells, and lifts her legs ready to jump. 'Go!'

Shane hits the skids.

She jumps, hitting the ground running, the bullock's tail in her hand.

A quick twist round her arm to get a good grip, and when the bullock's back legs come off the ground again, she pulls him sideways, and down he goes.

She's on the bullock's back before he can start kicking, grabs his hind leg and kneels on his rump, holding the leg high to immobilise him.

Shane turns the bike around and comes back. 'Shame they don't let girls do rodeo,' he says, lifting the bike onto its stand and pulling his belt off to tie the bullock's legs. 'You'd take out the steer wrestling no worries.'

'Shuddup.' Red turns her face away so he can't see her pride.

'It's true,' Shane says, finishing the loop.

'Let's go get the bull-catcher and come back for him.' Red steps off the bullock, gammon organised, efficient.

As they walk to the bike, they see the chopper hovering about a kilometre away.

'They're watching you,' Shane teases her.

'Get lost!' Red says, punching him hard on the arm. Her moment of sheer exhilaration, the joy she felt pitting her physical strength and skill against the bullock, is tainted now, public and vulnerable. She runs back to the bullock, undoes the belt and lets it go, *Maww, Maww,* to find its way back to the herd.

7

———

It's late when they finish the cattle. The sun is hanging like a huge red balloon out over the open country. The dust moves through the air like a lace curtain, making darker folds and crevices across the sky.

The cattle are in the yard waiting for drafting tomorrow. A killer's singled out and waiting in the race. Red and Shane sit on the top rail, the wood hard against their bum bones. Dad, Lofty and the others stand around talking, waiting for that half an hour, when the temperature drops a couple of degrees, the flies give up their endless search for food and there's still enough light to see.

It's time.

'Give us a hand here you two,' Dad yells.

Red jumps down and runs around to him.

Shane shows off, walking around on the top rail, arms outstretched like a tightrope walker, feet tingling.

'Get a move on, Shane.'

The shot rings loud in their ears. The beast crumples in a heap, is strung up, legs in the steel spreader, hung, cut. Dad and Lofty work, their knives slicing the skin away, loosening the tangle of guts so it falls like spaghetti, leaving a gaping red hole. They carve out the special cuts: heart, liver, kidney. Shane lays them on a tray in the back of the bull-catcher, covered with wet hessian.

The saw screams as they cut up the carcass, then lift the cut quarters and carry them over their shoulders to the chiller.

Red washes her favourite 'milk gut' under the tap and puts it in a flour-bag to take home.

Everyone goes up to the big house to have a muster barbecue. The anti-bug lights on the veranda cover everything with a yellow sheen. They eat kidney, liver, heart and thick slabs of eye fillet with plenty of salt.

Mum's cooking. She's laughing, light-headed. She loves musters. It makes her feel like that young girl she was twenty years ago, straight from high school, heading north to work outside in the warmth with the smell of cattle and dust. She rode everything flat-out in those days: horses, bikes, cars. She and Shane's dad fell in love on the stock camp and she stayed. They still laugh, teasing each other about whether she fell in love with the country, the man or his bull-catcher.

The barbecue is built out of two truck wheel rims, one on top of the other, a thick grill placed on top.

'Come on, eat you mad bugger,' Mum teases the young chopper pilot.

'What?' he reckons, gammon innocent.

Mum laughs. 'You're mad! You had that chopper doing three-sixties and back-flips.'

'That's not mad. Wanna come for a ride tomorrow?' he says with a sparkle in his eyes. 'I'll show you mad.'

'Twenty years ago maybe,' she laughs. 'Nowadays I'd be sick.'

'Good work with that bullock, Red,' the chopper pilot says to Red when she comes up to get some food.

She nods thanks and walks away, embarrassed.

'Don't be shy,' he says, offering her a beer.

Everyone stops talking.

'Doesn't drink!' Lofty says. His voice is loud in the silence.

'At fourteen I hope not!' Dad says, walking over.

'Fourteen? Big girl for fourteen.'

'Just keep your mouth shut, young fella, if you know what's good for you,' Dad says, touching the chopper pilot's arm and leading him back to the barbecue.

'Don't you worry about me,' the pilot laughs. 'I'm every father's nightmare.'

'Well, don't push it here, mate.' Dad's voice is serious.

'You get enough cattle?' the pilot asks, changing the subject.

'Has to be enough – that's all there is. Been that bloody dry this year.'

'Reevey was saying they want a five per cent increase on last year's muster.'

'What?'

Shane catches Red's eye and they slip away into the darkness. Once Dad starts on about the Company, he'll go on forever. After a few beers he'll be telling the whole sad story. How the place should have been his. His great-grandfather started the place. Built it up. His father brought in stud cattle. They were making money. Then the Company talked his father into making improvements. Got him to take out a loan

– to increase the profits, they said. To send his son Bill, to boarding school and then to Agricultural College. Buy the missus a new car – not safe driving that old truck to town. But they didn't like the bad years, did they? And in no time, they were calling in the loan. He'll tell them how the Company bought up most of the stations. How he had to take the job of manager just to stay on his land.

Shane and Red walk along the familiar path in the dark. Shane whistles to the dogs. 'Get up the front!' He sends them ahead to check for snakes.

The moon helps define the path, the sheds, Red's house. They walk past the cattle shuffling and moaning in the stock-yards and head out toward the floodplain paddock. The sky opens up around them from horizon to horizon, a deep darkness littered with thousands of sparkling jewels.

'Those old Europeans reckoned that the sky was a sieve and the stars were the sun shining through the holes.'

'Them old people reckon the stars are the spirits of dead people.'

They sit on the grass.

It's lighter out here. They can see clearly. Must be because it's more open for the light from the stars. Or there's more reflection space for the moon, perhaps. Sitting on the grass, they feel the chill lifting from the ground, the moisture of the morning dew already hanging in the air.

The floodplain buzz rings in their ears, bringing back the noise from the valley.

It was silly. They over-reacted. Both of them. All that happened was they took the wrong track and got disoriented. But for some reason they full-on panicked. Lost it.

Why?

They've been lost before plenty of times. They're always getting lost. What about that time down at Bog Swamp? They wandered around for hours, thin grey trees all around them, thick black mud up their knees. They never lost it then. They were scared but . . .

They sit side by side thinking about the valley. But they don't talk about it. The shame is still too raw. Red panicking, yelling out to the spirits in Language. Shane collapsing to the ground in fear. If they talk about it, those things would have to be said. They'd have to joke or tease each other. So they say nothing.

Just then the wind picks up behind them and they hear the chopper pilot's voice. It comes down to them as clear as if he were right there.

'Your boyfriend,' Shane teases.

'He's a good chopper pilot,' Red answers sharply.

Shane's suddenly wild, really wild. The music and chatter from the party hangs in his hurt, angry silence.

Then Red says, 'He's up himself,' and laughs, punching Shane in the arm to say, *Don't get all wild.*

And they lie down on the grass, hands behind their heads, legs bent, watching the stars.

8

___

'Should take the salt lick down the floodplain tonight,' Shane says.

'But—'

'Just to get them addicted – we can work out where to put the donkey trap later.'

They sit up, turn to look at the big house. Lots of noise and laughter still. They're all distracted. *No one's going to catch us tonight. This is the best chance we're gonna get.*

'C'mon.' Shane signals the dogs to get in behind and stay quiet. He and Red move quietly over the soft earth and down the path to the saddle shed, where the salt licks are kept. Shane goes straight in, stumbles over something. 'I can't see. Come and help me find it.'

'No way! There's rats in there.'

'You scared of rats, Red?'

'Shuddup.'

'Got it,' Shane says. *Thump! Crash!* He bumps into something else. 'Should have grabbed a torch.'

'Yeah, and Grandad would have seen us miles away.'

'Grandad would have seen what?' Lofty asks from the door in Language.

Shane and Red freeze.

'We were just going to—'

'Just give'it that horse salt—'

Kriol and Language tumble over each other, urgent words fill the air.

'You still trying to catch those horses? Even after today?' Lofty speaks again in Language.

Silence.

He knows?

'We're just going to put salt lick down on the floodplain,' Red says slowly, trying to think what they were going to do and coming up blank. *What was their plan*? 'We wanted to get the horses addicted to the salt lick and build a donkey trap around it. Maybe trap the mare and foal so they won't die.'

'They need the minerals to survive,' Shane says, speaking carefully, like he would to his father.

Silence.

Then, 'Grandfather, I want one of those mares,' Red says in Language.

Silence. A long silence.

'You are yourself,' Lofty answers finally, his voice soft with disappointment. 'When we walk in this country, we don't walk in a line. We walk separate – each one finds his own track.' He turns and walks away.

They stare at the dark space that held him.

'Now we're buggered,' Shane whispers. 'Why'd you tell him we went up there?'

'I didn't.'

'So how does he know?'

Red ignores his question. 'We going to take this down to

the floodplain or what?' Grabbing the salt lick from Shane, she goes outside and heads off down the path.

'What about Lofty?'

'Didn't say we couldn't go, did he?' Red walks away.

'But . . . Wait. Hang on!' Shane holds the oldest dog to stay with them, and hunts the others. 'Get back up to the house.'

They stand looking at him.

'Go on.'

They go, turning back every now and then to see if he really means it, and he has to hunt them again with a flick of his arm and a growl.

Shane signals the old dog to heel and he and Red walk past Red's house without looking in. They know Lofty's sitting by the fire and they don't want to face him. As they get farther from the yards the sounds of talking and laughing float down from the big house.

The moon is high now, bathing the world with silver. Tiny sparkles of light reflect on wolf spiders' eyes and the dewdrops caught on webs strung between blades of grass. The on-off, on-off light of fireflies flickers here and there, and the air fills with thousands of insect noises as they leave the fence-line and walk onto the floodplain proper.

'This will do,' Red says.

'No, farther. They won't come up this high.'

'We might scare them off if we get too close.'

Shane starts to answer, hears a noise, stops and grabs the dog. His voice comes out: 'A . . . a . . . shhh.'

Red stifles a giggle and steps around him.

'Shhh.' Shane grabs Red's shirt, his hands resting on her shoulders from behind. They stand still, listening.

There's the shiver of a horse shaking itself, its skin rattling over bone. The old dog starts to growl.

'Shhh.' Shane lays his hand on the dog's head. 'Shut up.' His voice is quiet but serious.

A soft growl, then silence.

They can hear the horses clearly now, walking, biting, ripping the grass. Crouching down, Red puts the salt lick on the thick dry grass. Then they can see them, the horses: just a movement, not even an outline. Just shapes, but it's them for sure, drifting across the open land like ghosts in a mist. The foal is under his mother's flank. *There's the stallion. Look at the size of him, at least two hands bigger than the mares.*

The horses come closer. *Lie down.* Red pulls Shane's shirt and they lie flat in the grass. Mozzies whine in their ears and bite through their shirts where the material pulls tight across their shoulders. The mist is almost white in the moonlight, the horses' snorts and shivers muffled in its thickness. Their dark shapes are clear now, so clear you can see the softness of their lips lifting and curving while they chew, the shapely curve of their fetlocks as they lift them to slap insects away.

Red and Shane snuggle down as low as possible. The grey light blends them into the grass. The horses come right up: twenty-seven of them, heads down biting at the dry grass, *crunch, crunch,* shaking off mozzies, *swish, swish,* their tails singing through the air. So close you could reach out a hand and touch a fetlock, the warm softness of a nose.

And then they're gone.

Shane and Red close their eyes to hear better, till the sound of them fades too. They lie quiet on the grass long after that, wallowing in remembering, until Red pulls at Shane's shirt to say *Let's go, I'm getting eaten alive* and they leopard-crawl back to the fence. Finding their way by the light of the fire they walk back to Lofty's, still numb with the magic and memory.

. . .

Lofty is sitting by the fire, smouldering with resentment.

They sit down beside him.

He keeps looking at the fire, ignoring them.

Shane turns his hand over to ask Red what they should do.

Red shrugs her shoulders. She's never seen Lofty so angry before.

'Early start in the morning,' Lofty says sending Shane home. 'Got to get all them cattle drafted tomorrow.'

Red changes and crawls into bed.

Lofty stays by the fire in silence.

'Grandfather,' Red calls softly from her bed in Language, trying to soothe his anger. 'We met the horses on the flood-plain. They came so close they breathed our smell. They breathed the same air as us.'

Silence.

'It could be time for him to come back to humans, that horse. Mightbe he's been wild for long enough.'

'Mightbe,' Lofty says, uncommitted.

'Grandfather, tell me the story about my mother.'

Lofty is silent for a long time, then he turns in his chair to face her and speaks to her in Language. 'The day your mother was born we were moving cattle from Woolnamurra,' he says. 'Your grandmother was keeping up the rear.' In his mind he can still see her, her huge pregnant belly sticking out over the pommel of the saddle. 'Your grandmother stopped and waited for your mother to come under that wajarri tree there. But your mother took too long, your grandmother was so tired when your mother was born, that old horse had to sniff your mother and lick her new birth blood to clean her and give her breath. When your grandmother brought her to meet us at supper camp, your mother was already looking around laughing to be up so high. She knew the smell of horses from that first day. She could talk to the horses. They wanted to please her. She was a good stockman, better than anyone.'

When Shane gets back to the house Mum's still cleaning up. He'd like to tell her about the horses. She would love to see them. But she'd have to tell Dad, and Dad said he'd shoot Roman if he came anywhere near the station mares. So he grabs a plastic bag and helps her collect the rubbish. 'What's the matter with Lofty?' he asks.

'That silly cocky young pilot.'

'He's right up himself.'

Silence. Shane feels silly. Shouldn't have said that. Sounds like he's jealous or something.

'Shane. You and Red.'

'What?'

'It's just—'

'Mum, we're just friends. It's that stupid chopper pilot, not me.'

She looks at him, thinking, sizing him up. Is he old enough for this conversation? 'There was a time when Aboriginal women weren't safe—' she starts.

'Mum, I'm not listening.'

She says no more, but the truth of it hangs around him in the night air, and the memory of Red so close on the floodplain.

9

_____

In his dreams Shane is out on the floodplain, a herd of horses in the mist around him. *He runs his hand along their backs as they walk past, feeling the hardness of their muscles, the smell of them sharp in his nose. A mare nuzzles her head under his arm. There are soft murmurings of Language. People on horseback. Long shapes of men walking beside them, the tips of their spear bundles showing above their heads. Shane walks with them, calls out softly, is answered. He falls deeper into sleep.*

It's a dark night. Dingoes are hunting on the floodplain, their eyes bright as they slip through the bush, their soft pads silent. The horses suddenly smell them. They try to run but they are surrounded. They huddle in a circle, snorting, stamping, their eyes wide. One at time the dingoes slip in, snapping at fetlocks.

The mother steps over her foal, keeping him beneath her, kicking out at the dogs.

Ducking under the flying hoofs, a dingo bites the foal. The foal panics. Runs out from under his mother. The dogs leap to knock him over, and they're all over him in a snarling mass, ripping him to pieces.

Shane jerks awake, sweat cold on his skin. Everything's black – black and silent. Then, *Ooooww!* A howl rises to a peak and echoes down from the stone country. Dingoes. *The foal!* He jumps up. The blackness seeps in through the fly-wire surrounding him. There's no moon. *The dingoes are hunting. They could get the foal, easy.*

Silence. No birds yet – too early.

Ooooww! rises up again. The dingoes are still up in the stone country. *Please, please, please, let the horses still be down on the floodplain. Please don't let the foal die.*

He lies listening, waiting. Can't do anything now. Go back to sleep.

But he can't.

Wait. Wait.

Eventually, through the fly-wire, the tall gums come into shape as the morning sky turns grey. *Should go and check. If they've killed the foal, hawks will be circling over the body at first light. But we're drafting today! Starting early!* He looks out at the sky to check the time. *Yep. Enough time if you hurry.*

He slips quickly out of bed, his bare feet silent on the floorboards. He slept in his clothes – always does when it's an early start. Saves fumbling round in the dark. Just have to get up, grab boots, hat, belt, and he's ready to go. His bedroom is a fly-wired section of the veranda. He walks carefully, knowing the way in the dark, soft morning light marking the edges, the cupboard, the door, where the veranda drops away, the collection of bridles hanging on coat hooks against the wall.

The dogs greet him with wild jumps at the bottom of the steps.

'Shh. Get lost,' he whispers, pushing them away as he sits to put his boots on. They wait, tails thumping the ground, little excited whines escaping from their closed mouths and, when he stands, they run in front of him along the path to the stockyards.

Red wakes in the darkness; hears boots padding on earth – *what's that? Someone going down the yards. Shane. Has to be Shane. What's he doing?* She lifts the mozzie net and climbs out of bed, grabs her jeans and wraps a blanket around herself against the cold.

Lofty's snores stop. He's listening.

'Hey!' Red calls out to Shane, asking him what's going on.

'Nothing. You right,' he says as he walks past.

She pulls her jeans on under her dress and follows him, her bare feet silent, cold in the dew on the dry grass. 'Hear them dingoes?' she asks.

'Yeah.'

'The horses'll be down on the floodplain,' she says, guessing that's where he's going, telling him that the foal's okay, that he shouldn't worry.

'Can you hear them?' Shane asks, and they both stop and listen.

'Nothing.'

Cattle moan in the stockyards. Old Milkjug, Mum's house-cow, bawls. Her udder is full and painful. Mum separates her from her calf all night so there's plenty of milk when she milks her in the morning. *Bawww!* the calf yells, crawling to his feet, thirsty.

'They reckon you going to milk them,' Red laughs.

'As if,' Shane says, gammon real tough.

· · ·

They lean into the stockyard rails and Shane whistles. Chocolate answers with a neigh and trots up to meet him. He leans down and slips through the rails. Chocolate puts her head under his arm, pushing against him to say hello. Shane rubs his hand along her neck and through her straight-up-in-the-air mane.

She's part Timor pony. Her hoofs are sure and careful. She never trips. Like the *Man from Snowy River's* horse, Shane reckons. He rests his hand on her shoulder, holding a handful of mane, and swings up on her back in a smooth movement.

'Where you going?' Red asks.

'Just to have a look.'

'Wait. I'm coming.'

'Nah – take too long to get a horse up. Wait here. Won't be long.'

'You'll scare them!'

'I'm going bareback. They won't smell me. I'll stay back.'

Red walks over the soft ground to open the gate.

'Thanks. Can you hold the dogs?' Shane trots through the gate and out into the greyness. 'See ya.'

'Come here!' Red calls the dogs, her voice stern. 'Sid-down!' The dogs obey, sitting at her heels in the shadows, watching the dark shape of Shane disappear beneath the lightening sky.

Red wraps her blanket tight around herself and walks back home, her chest so swollen with tears it hurts. Life is so unfair. Lofty grunts good morning. She puts the billy over the fire to boil. He looks at her to ask, *What's the matter?*

She shrugs her shoulders. *No use talking to you, she thinks, her head down. You don't subbie anything. How would you like to be left behind all the time? If I had a smart horse I could've gone. But no. I have to ride a myall stock-horse. No way he would come to a whistle like that. Have to chase him all over the place and corner him to catch him. He spins round and threatens to kick you once he's cornered, and bites and bucks and pig-roots for the first half hour after you get on. Then he shies at anything that moves. You reckon riding the myall horses will make me a good horse-woman? I am a good horsewoman. Well haven't you noticed? How good do I have to be?*

She glares toward Lofty's bed. She wants to yell at him. But she can't. She sits down by the fire, smarting with injustice, slapping her hair off her face. Her eyes narrow. *I'm going to catch one of those mares, she thinks, crossing her fingers. Please let them have got into the salt lick. They will definitely come back for more once they've tasted it.*

Lofty watches Red. *You're a good girl Redeleenia, he thinks. A smart girl. Clever like your grandmother. Good stockwoman too, like your mother and your grandmother. But you've got that cheeky streak in there. Pushing all the boundaries – never take no for an answer.* He sits up, lifting the mozzie net over behind him.

They sit in silence.

'Grandad,' Red says in Language.

Lofty looks at the ground for a long time.

'Nykuli.' She says his Bunuba name, thinking he might not have heard her.

'We'll talk after, later,' he says. 'Get ready for drafting.'

10

———

The morning is cold. Up high on Chocolate, Shane watches the land come to life. Birds flit from branch to branch, calling; a line of geese is silhouetted against the grey sky; the skeletal shapes of gum trees come into focus.

He leans forward and Chocolate lifts into a canter. He has trained her so his knees and the shift of his weight give her clear instructions. She'll jump to a full gallop from a standstill if he says 'C'mon' and leans right forward. She'll brake so quick her back legs sit under her like a dog's if he leans right back. She'll spin on a sixpence. All he has to do is lean to one side and dig his heels in.

Shane sits back now to prove himself right, and Chocolate slows to a fast trot. She's a good horse – quick and smart – but . . . *Roman. If I could catch Roman, imagine . . .* Then he feels suddenly guilty, disloyal, and pats Chocolate. 'Hey, Red could have you instead of that wild old stock-horse she rides.' Then, with his tone serious, he makes a pledge, 'If I catch Roman, I promise I'll give you to Red.'

. . .

The sun isn't yet over the horizon. Down on the floodplain the mist hangs in soft swirls over the magnetic termite mounds. They look like dark sentries against the grey sky. The ground crackles underfoot, thick matted couch grass.

There's the salt lick. They've been at it, worn one side down already. *Yes!*

The horses are over on the other side of the floodplain, heads down, eating, slowly wandering back toward the stone country.

They're downwind. *Better be quick*, Shane thinks. *They'll smell us any minute and bolt.* 'Stand up. Stand up,' he says as he lifts his legs up to stand on Chocolate's back.

There he is, the stallion. There's the foal, jumping, rearing and bouncing in the cool morning air. 'Stand up,' Shane says, telling Chocolate to keep still. She's nervous, not sure what to do with Shane in this strange position.

At that moment the sun peeps over the hills behind the horses, covering everything in golden light. It's beautiful. The grazing horses, the dew sparkling like jewels on the grass, the dark spikes and turrets of the stone country and the sky the palest blue above. Shane holds his breath, caught by this moment – wanting to hold it forever like a photograph.

Then Roman throws his head up, nostrils flaring, smelling the air, snorting to clear his nose.

Oh no! Now they're going to bolt!

But Roman stands still, calls out.

The mares look up to see who it is and go back to eating.

Chocolate answers with a soft whinny.

Roman starts trotting toward Shane and Chocolate. A lazy trot, holding each leg aloft before putting it down and lifting the next one. Like a Spanish dancing horse, his tail high, his head up, calling out as he comes.

Shane's blood runs quick with excitement. He sits down on Chocolate's back. *I should move off. What if he attacks?* But the big horse is so majestic, he's mesmerised. Shane can't help but stay, watching and watching.

Roman stops about twenty metres away, calling, throwing his head back. He's almost gold in the morning sun.

Chocolate nods her head up and down, neighing.

Roman dances forward, tossing his head in the air. *Chocolate's in season!* Shane realises. *What if Roman hunts Chocolate back to his herd? How would I stop him. Chocolate hasn't even got a bridle on.* 'Come on,' he says, leaning forward, urging her away.

She turns and walks a little, looking back at Roman.

'C'mon! Let's get out of here!' Shane yells, kicking her sides to get her going.

But she won't go any faster, and Roman's right there now, lifting his front legs, squealing, dancing around, trying to touch noses.

'C'mon! C'mon!' Shane sits right forward, kicking Chocolate's sides till she finally starts to trot.

Roman stops.

Chocolate slows down, calls back. She wants to stay with him. She stops.

Roman looks back at the mares on the floodplain. They're still eating. He calls out to them. They lift their heads, acknowledge him, and go back to eating. He wants to go back and take them to safety, but he wants to follow Chocolate. The two horses face each other, ten metres between them.

'C'mon girl. C'mon. Let's go,' Shane urges. Chocolate takes a step away.

Roman takes a step to follow.

Chocolate takes another step.

So does Roman.

Hey, Shane thinks. *Would he follow Chocolate? It's only two hundred metres to the hessian fence and then into the laneway. If I kept her really close to him, maybe he'll follow and I can trap him in the laneway. Please, please let him come.*

So Shane lets Chocolate be. She responds quickly, turning to face Roman.

Roman answers but doesn't move.

C'mon! Come! Shane wills the big horse in his mind.

He urges Chocolate toward the fence, keeping a couple of metres' distance between them.

Roman follows slowly, calling to her, rearing on the spot.

The sun's up. They'll be drafting by now. *Dad's going to be angry. Hope Dad doesn't come roaring down here in the bull-catcher to look for me.*

Roman is following but Shane's body is tense with worry. *Don't let anything happen to make him bolt. A snake in their path, the dogs. What if the dogs come looking for him and scare him off?*

But they don't.

Metre by metre, Shane and Chocolate entice the big horse toward the laneway.

The hessian fence. They can see the hessian fence clearly now. *Keep him real close. If Roman sees the fence he'll bolt for sure.* Chocolate stops as if reading his mind. *Hey, hang on, don't let him get too close.* The huge stallion's right there, reaching out to nip at Chocolate.

The hairs on Shane's neck lift. Beneath him he can feel Chocolate hesitating. It's hard for her to keep moving away. She wants to stop. 'C'mon,' he whispers to her. 'Just a little bit farther.' They move like itchy grubs, slowly edging their way toward the laneway.

Don't smell the yards yet, Shane begs, thankful that the wind's behind them.

They go into the long yard and through the wide cocky gate – a length of fence that can be easily dragged to one side to make a gate, then pulled back into place once the animals are through.

Now what? Now we're in the laneway, what?

Got to get that gate closed somehow. But I can't get off. That'll spook him for sure.

Red. Where the hell's Red when you want her?

There's Shane, the idiot. Red stands up to yell, *You've got us both in big trouble! What the hell has taken you so long?* But she sees two horses. One behind the other. The sun's bright behind them, so she can't quite make them out. *That's Chocolate and it's the stallion! Is the stallion attacking Shane and Chocolate!? No. They'd be flat out galloping if he was attacking them.* The horses come closer, closer, till she can see Shane.

He waves her round, signalling to her to close the gate. *He's going to trap the stallion!*

She covers her face with her hands for a minute to calm her racing mind, then runs around the long way to the bottom of the laneway, bent over so the big horse can't see her, and pulls the cocky gate closed.

He's caught.

Shane urges Chocolate over to the fence, slips off her back and steps through the wire fence. He ducks down and rushes back to where Red's waiting, crouched on the ground.

Roman's snorting and stamping, trying to nip Chocolate. She's playfully kicking out at him, keeping just out of his reach. The stallion hasn't noticed he's trapped.

'The old man's looking for you,' Red says. 'We're both in deep trouble.'

'Have they started already?'

'They're waiting for us. You're getting a flogging.'

'Quick!' They run up along the fence to the cattle yards.

11

———

'Where've you two been!' Dad yells at them over the roar of the bull-catcher. 'Get in there quick and push that first mob through.'

Red and Shane call the dogs to come and hunt the cattle into the race.

The cattle bawl as they're separated from the mob, and baulk with fear as they're forced to go through gates and steel tunnels.

The dew dries quickly and hundreds of hoofs lift the dust thick into the air. Shane pulls a hanky from his pocket to wrap around his nose and mouth. Red narrows her eyes and pulls the brim of her hat down.

Dogs bark, cattle rush past, wild-eyed.

Lofty's up on the rails, directing.

Cut that one off!

Send that one through!

The sun climbs higher, pressing the heat down on them. Dust sticks to sweat, gritty between clothes and skin.

They stop, sit on the rails, slug water from the waterbag, rest for a few minutes and go back to work.

'Bulumana! Cleanskin!' Lofty yells from the top of the rails as a young bull comes rushing through the gate. Two, three years old. Wild. Never been caught, branded or castrated.

Red pushes the crush gate forward to cut him off.

'Push him up! Push him up!' Shane yells to the dogs, and they rush in to nip and send him through into the isolation pen.

Neat. Red and Shane smile at each other. *Good work.*

But before they can get the gate closed the bull spins round, head down, slashing at the dogs with his horns, snot spinning out in an arc from his nose. The dogs squeal and duck out of the way.

The bull sees Red and charges.

Two quick steps and she's at the top of the rails with the bull standing, wild-eyed, beneath her.

Everyone laughs.

Lofty's proud.

'Nearly got ya,' Shane teases, and the bull turns on him, chasing him up the rails. He's in the round yard, trotting around, hooking his horns at everything.

'Leave him quiet,' Lofty says.

But Shane wants to get the drafting over quickly and get back to Roman. So he gammons he doesn't hear and sends the dogs in to push him back into the isolation pen.

The bull rushes at the dogs, smashing into the stockyard rails, cutting his face. He spins around – blood, dust and snot, front legs spread, ready to charge.

'Get out,' Red yells at the dogs, but they can't stop, they're beyond listening, wanting to rip and tear, to taste blood.

They rush in.

The young bull jumps, his huge body lifting higher than is possible. Front legs over the rails, scrambling, back legs dangle, he seesaws for a moment, and then topples over to the other side in a heap. He crawls to his feet and bolts out over the open country.

Shane and Red stare at each other in disbelief. Neither of them is game to look up at Lofty. They don't want to see the 'I told you so' look on his face. But before he sends the dogs back to work, Shane calls them over, making them sit, quietening them down, cooling their lust for blood.

It's afternoon before all the cattle are through the crush into the truck and ready to leave.

Dad's climbing along the top of the truck making adjustments to the cattle: turning this one, prodding that one, making them stand close together so they can't lie down and get trampled to death.

Lofty's cutting up wood. The axe swings and falls and he feeds the kindling to a small cooking fire at the edge of a huge mound of ash. There's been more than fifty years of cooking fires in this one spot, under the shade of a big old tree. Big logs surround it for seats. A griller on one side. When they get a killer, sometimes they'll grill the milk gut, liver, kidneys and heart fresh from the bullock, smelling rich and acrid. At branding time, when the air's thick with burning hair and their mouths are salty with the smell of blood, Lofty grills calves' testes into little brown balls – sweetbreads they call them – beautiful. Make your farts really stink, though.

Red, Shane and Lofty drink hot tea, blowing the flies away from their mouths before they sip. The wind whips up the dust around them and runs with it across the open land. Dad comes over and pours his tea, pushing the brim of his hat back, showing his forehead white against his burnt face.

'That should keep the Company happy for a couple of hours,' he tells Lofty. They laugh. 'Don't know what we're supposed to breed from if they sell all the cattle. Bunch of idiots.'

Lofty nods, agreeing.

'Caught Roman this morning,' Shane says.

'What, mate?' Dad asks, not listening.

'I caught that stallion, Roman, this morning. He's down in the laneway.'

Dad looks at Lofty to ask if it's true.

Lofty shrugs his shoulders and looks at Red.

Red nods. 'He's there. I shut the cocky gate.'

Dad laughs, his face crinkled up, and opens his hands to say *How? What happened?*

'He followed me.'

'What?'

Shane looks at him, nodding his head.

'True? Got to have a look at this.' They all jump in the bull-catcher and drive right round, coming up along the bottom fence so they don't scare the horses. There's the cocky gate closed, and there they are, Roman and Chocolate, standing together like old mates.

'That's him now,' Lofty says.

'That's him all right. How?'

'Chocolate's in season. He just followed her.'

'You're joking.' Dad laughs and laughs, loud. 'They had half the country looking for this mongrel horse and he follows you home like a starving pup?' He pushes Shane's head, laughing. 'You're unbelievable.'

'Red helped too.'

'The pair of you. You're bloody winners.' Dad is smiling so hard they can't see his eyes.

'Can I keep him?'

'I'd say so. Killiara's changed hands a couple of times since then. Can't see anyone would even know about him over there now.'

They sit watching the two horses. Roman's rubbing his face along Chocolate's neck. She's leaning into his caress.

'Let's push him up and have a look.'

'But . . . ' Shane says, remembering the bull. 'What if he panics?'

'It'll be right, son. We'll take him slow.'

The bull-catcher moves forward. Roman stands still, head high, snorting. Chocolate turns and walks up the laneway toward the yards. Roman sees the fence, the yards ahead, lifts both front legs and bounces first one way and then the other, his back legs crouching.

'God, look at him,' Shane says. 'He must have been some cutting horse.'

Dad slows the bull-catcher to a stop and waits.

Roman turns, prancing, lifting his legs high, his nose right up, mane flowing out behind him. He seems uncon-nected to the ground, as if he might just fly.

'Reckon we should put some other horses in with him? To calm him down?'

'He'll be right.'

'But Dad, what if he panics and goes straight over the fence?'

'We'll take it slow.'

Slower! Slower! Shane wills his dad as the bull-catcher moves toward the horses. He feels like vomiting, his gut is so empty. Then he realises he's holding his breath, and gulps some air.

Red grabs Shane's shirt, holding it tight. 'Don't panic. Don't panic,' she tells the big horse.

Chocolate and Roman move slowly up the laneway, Roman almost dancing on the spot, Chocolate trotting, lazy, her head down.

Then they're in the holding pen, a high steel cable fence surrounding them, so Dad speeds up a bit.

'Dad, he'll go straight over.'

'Calm down, will ya.'

The bull-catcher stops and Shane and Red jump out. They walk so slowly, their steps so deliberate, trying not to frighten the horses, that it feels like they're in slow motion.

They close the gate. The stallion is locked in, caught. They stand holding on to the gate, watching, delight and disbelief making their brains numb.

Shane looks at Red and smiles, the whites of his eyes and his teeth pale against his dusty face. She laughs and grabs him in a hug, bending back to pull him up off the ground. He goes to yell but, remembering the horses, he clamps his mouth down and grabs her arms, dancing around in a circle. They laugh with their smiles and their movements.

Behind them Lofty and Dad watch the stallion in silence, the jerking bubble of the bull-catcher humming in their ears and rattling their bones.

12

Dad drives the bull-catcher up closer to the fence and turns the motor off.

Shane and Red turn to look at him, shocked. From the time Dad starts the bull-catcher in the morning, that engine never stops. It goes all day. He jumps out to move stuff, to work on a fence, to grab a calf or close a gate, but whatever he does, the bull-catcher is always bubbling away in the background.

Roman realises he's trapped and rears up, singing out, calling in anger and frustration, then high-steps round and round the yard, tail floating out behind him.

Dad sits in the bull-catcher, his leg out on the running board, his body leaning forward over the steering wheel, looking at Roman. *That's like me,* he thinks. *Running scared. Running around in circles trying to stay on the country, my country, trying to please the Company so we can live where I was born. Tomorrow there's a big meeting. All the Company stations have to come together so some shiny-bum businessman can lecture them on 'returns on investment', 'marketplace growth', 'expansion'.*

Expansion! You can't increase the amount of cattle, you idiots, unless you increase the amount of land.

Roman rears again, screaming out his rage.

'Get used to it, mate,' Dad says. 'You're trapped just like the rest of us.'

'Open the top gate. Push 'em up the round yard,' Lofty says.

Shane opens the gate, and Red calls out to hunt the horses through into the round yard. This is where Roman will stay, to be trained.

'Leave him quiet now,' Lofty says.

Shane starts to fill the water trough – the horses haven't drunk all day.

'Nomore,' Lofty says. 'Leave it.'

Shane looks at him to ask, *Why?*

'Give him water morning-time. He can't find water for himself now, only you can find it for him.'

Chocolate rushes over and sips the small puddle, looking at Shane to ask for more.

Shane pats her. 'Sorry, girl, you have to wait too.'

Dad starts the bull-catcher and goes up to the big house.

Lofty wanders back to his camp. 'Go open that cocky gate you mob.'

Red and Shane race down to open the gate and come straight back to the horses.

And they're still there in the late afternoon, sitting on the top rail watching the horses in the yellow light.

Chocolate comes over, nudging Shane and then Red. Red drops from the rail and Chocolate rubs her face along Red's arm. Pushing her hard, asking for water and food.

'Nomore. Tomorrow,' Red says. 'I'll bring you some flash hay.'

Shane has a pang of sorrow. He's gonna have to do it. He promised himself he would. But . . . *No buts about it. Red deserves her, she's the right size. They'll work well together.* 'Red, you can have Chocolate.'

'Really?'

He nods. 'Got Roman now.'

Red smiles and wraps her arms around Chocolate's neck. Roman watches Red and calls out to Chocolate, worried. He is standing in one place for the first time since he came into the yards, but his body is shaking, his legs lifting, eyes bright with fear.

And as the sun goes down, Shane and Red are still on the stockyard rails, talking, watching the horses, their hats and boots silhouetted against the pink sky.

Chocolate leans against Roman, nipping his neck with her lips. He ignores her, never taking his eyes off Shane and Red. Even when it's dead dark, and Shane and Red have to go in, Roman stands watching, listening as their footfalls disappear into the night.

Shane lies in bed on his back, excited, his mind racing. *Got to get up first thing in the morning and start working Roman. Dad, Mum and Lofty will be away at the big Company meeting. I'm gonna to do all the training myself,* he thinks. *So he becomes a one-man horse. A horse that won't let anyone else ride, pat, feed or do anything for him. I'll have all morning, hours of time on my own with him; I won't have to listen to Dad or Lofty. I'll stand in the middle of the round yard and get him going around. Got to get communication happening, make him face up.*

He remembers Dad's lessons. *When they turn their back on you, they're treating you like the predator – defending themselves. You got to get them to face you – to trust you. Get eye contact and keep it. But, most important, you got to read them, know what they're going to do before they know it themselves.*

Then Shane's dreaming. *He's in the round yard, the big horse facing up. He's touching him, feeling his skin trembling under his fingers.*

Red cuts a couple of pieces of roast beef from the camp-oven and spoons the rich dark gravy over it. Lofty's sitting on his kero tin by the fire.

Red's so happy. *Chocolate. Chocolate's mine.* She eats quickly. 'You should have seen it, Grandad,' she says in Language. 'That stallion just followed Chocolate. He's in love, he didn't even see us. I bolted down and shut up that gate. We got him. Never thought a wild horse would do that.'

'There's weakness in everyone.'

Red looks at him. *He's sad, really sad. He didn't want Shane to catch that horse.* 'Grandad, why didn't you tell Shane about Jandamarra?'

'That's not his story.'

'What do you mean? He comes from here. He was born here.'

Lofty turns his head away, looking out into the dark.

'You always say, "Same country, same blood",' she continues. 'You cut a white and a black person, they both got red blood inside them.'

'Same blood, but different history,' Lofty says in Language. 'Shane's family comes to this place from a different road.' His tone says the conversation's finished.

Red eats her dinner and crawls into bed. 'Tell me the story about Jandamarra. That one about when he took all the people to safety in the high country.'

Lofty moves his chair around closer to her bed and tells her the story in Language. 'Jandamarra was a police tracker,' he says, starting the story as he has a hundred times. 'He can find anyone.' He tells Red how Jandamarra worked for the policeman, Richardson. Their job was to clean the country so that white men could raise cattle. How Jandamarra and the policeman went out and rounded up all the people: women and children, strong men, clever men, magic men. 'Even the great man Ellemarra, they caught him.' How they put chains around the people's necks and legs and brought them to the police station. How the policeman left the people sitting out in the sun. 'They were getting sick, poor things,' Lofty says, 'Jandamarra asked the policeman Richardson to let the people go and sit in the shade. But the policeman said no.' Lofty sits in silence for a long time. Then he tells Red how Jandamarra and the policeman Richardson fought. How Jandamarra killed the policeman, grabbed all his guns and bullets, and escaped with the people back into the high country.

'So now the Government calls a meeting,' Lofty says. 'The malngarri are screaming. One man's face is red, white spit at the corner of his mouth. His eyes are so blue you can't see anything in there – they're empty. "We got to kill all the blackfellas", the man says. All the men and women and children. Everyone. We'll get Aboriginal people from other country to come and help us kill them.'

Lofty pauses. *Is Red asleep yet?*

'So now they call police trackers from Queensland and the Northern Territory to help them hunt all the people out of the country,' he continues. 'But still they can't get Jandamarra. It isn't like before. Jandamarra has bullets now, and guns. Jandamarra and his men ambush the policemen and trackers and kill them. If they make a camp, Jandamarra sneaks into that camp in the night, never touching the ground to leave tracks. He comes in like a bird and takes their guns and their food and spooks their horses. One time they come with lots of policemen and . . .' He stops.

Red is asleep, her breathing slow and heavy. Lofty tucks the mozzie net in under her mattress and goes back to the fire. Roman calls out from the round yard and Lofty's chest swells with emotion. 'But Jandamarra too had a weakness . . .' he says softly to the night.

13

'Shane! Shane! What're ya doing?' Red yells.

Shane wakes up with a jolt, hot and sweating. It's late.

'You gonna let them horses die of thirst?' she says, her face angry, contorted through the fly-wire door. She storms off, her bare feet thumping on the wooden floor.

Shane jumps out of bed and runs into the house. Mum and Dad have gone. The meeting. They went ages ago, taking Lofty with them. The house is silent. 'You idiot!' he says aloud. 'You've wasted all this time!' He drags on his clothes and runs down the steps, forgetting his boots. He has to go back up to get them.

The dogs jump up and lick his hands, bouncing in front of him.

'Get lost!' He kicks out at them, running to the yards.

Red's there already, swinging the axe with furious blows, a pile of kindling around her feet. *She better not have given them horses water*, he thinks, knowing how selfish it sounds as soon as he thinks it. *How bad is that? Making the horses go thirsty because you sleep in.*

The troughs are still empty. Red's right there, but they don't speak. He turns on the tap. Chocolate rushes over, her flanks high with thirst. She drinks quickly in great long sucks. They can see the water sliding up her neck.

Roman doesn't move.

They wait.

Still he doesn't move.

They should walk away, Shane knows that. He should move away and let the big horse drink. Let him get used to the yards, let him quieten down. Wait till he gets used to having people around and knows they won't hurt him. But Shane wants to get in before Dad and Lofty come back. He wants at least to get Roman close, get him to come up and make contact. Perhaps touch him.

Chocolate's full now. She turns and calls out to Roman.

He answers but stays still, absolutely still.

'Good girl. Good girl,' Shane says. 'Tell him it's okay. That we won't hurt him.' He grabs his rope and climbs through the fence, pats Chocolate right along her body, and walks out to stand in the middle of the round yard.

Roman watches.

'Big horse. Come on. You right.' Got to get him to see me, to start communicating.

Roman nods his head and moves forward.

Good, really good. The hardest thing to do is get the horse to face up. And Roman's doing it straight away – excellent!

Then suddenly Roman lays his ears back and rushes at him, teeth bared.

Shane lifts the rope and slaps the horse across the face, jumping backwards. Roman spins around and kicks out, both legs at once, *whack! whack!*, bouncing backwards between kicks, trying to hit what he missed first time.

Shane throws himself sideways, spinning into a half cart-wheel, and bolts for the rails.

Red laughs and laughs, leaning over laughing. 'That horse don't like you,' she says, and looks around for someone to tell. There's no one to tell so she just laughs some more.

'Shuddup.' Shane punches her on the arm, but he has to smile. It must have looked pretty funny.

They sit and watch the horses, looking at each other and smiling every now and then. 'Face it. He don't like you.'

'I'll get him. He's got to come and get a drink soon,' Shane says, trying to restore some pride.

Roman's thirsty. Really thirsty. One-and-a-half days without water. His body is weakening; an ache spreads across his fore-head, dulling his thinking. He needs to drink. The water's right there. The sunlight sparkles silver on the edge of the drops as they fall from the tap. The silken ripples move out from the impact, calling him. His mouth is so dry, saliva is caked white against his tongue. He can't swallow, his neck is sore, his guts high. The emptiness of thirst makes him feel like he's floating.

He takes a step forward.

Red and Shane freeze, holding their breath, begging, *Yes, c'mon, c'mon.*

And step by step Roman lifts his feet and places them one in front of the other.

Shane leans down real slow to pick up his rope.

Roman stops.

'Whatcha doing?' Red whispers though closed lips.

Shane doesn't answer. He stays bent until Roman, his eyes fixed on the rippling water, moves forward again.

Shane slowly stands, lifting the rope up.

Roman stops, staring. He can't see exactly what Shane is doing behind the rails but he knows it is dangerous. He waits. After five long minutes he starts to inch forward again.

Shane carefully spreads a loop, wrapping the rope around the rails to anchor it and taking the lasso through to hang down innocently inside the rails. Then he stands still, absolutely still.

The big horse comes closer. His thirst, and the humans as still as trees, make him daring. He knows the smell of rope and leather and the danger they pose, but the water is so close now. His nostrils flare as they fill with the sweet scent. Then the water is cool on his lips. He sucks its wetness in, washing the caked saliva from his mouth, drawing the sparkling water up in huge sucks. He closes his eyes for a second.

And *flick!* the lasso spreads in a circle above his head.

The whistle of the rope, the shadow across the water, don't register in Roman's mind, washed as it is in the quenching coolness of the water, till the rope hits back of his neck.

He jerks his head up, catching the rope behind his ears.

Shane flicks the rope down and the loop zips up tight under the horse's chin.

Roman screams, rearing into the air, eyes wild, hoofs lashing out.

The rope tightens, stiff between the rail and his neck.

As the horse comes down, Shane loosens the loop around the rail to pull it tighter, to bring him closer. But Roman jerks away before he can tighten it, before he can get his fingers round the rope properly. Roman jerks the rope and it burns through Shane's fingers, ripping the skin off. Stinging. He can't stop his fingers from opening, letting go. Letting the rope run. The coils beneath his feet whip up, around his leg. Caught! His leg's caught, reefed up and smashed against the rail! The horse jumps, jerks, pulls. *Crack! Crack! Crack!* Bone and skin smash into wood.

Darkness looms above him. Shane lifts his hands up to protect himself. Red grabs the axe, raises it above her head and crack. Thwang! Wood splinters. The rope whips through the air. Roman flips over backwards.

Shane collapses. His leg is stuck out, stiff. He can't move it. His jeans are torn and bloody. A cut above his eye starts to dribble blood.

Roman scrabbles, tangled in the rope for a minute, then he's up, running, his head to one side keeping the rope out of his way. His body bouncing, his eyes wide, the rope loosened around his neck.

Shane leans back against the rails, his face twisted with pain. Red's feeling his leg, trying to see if it's broken. She looks towards the house, but the Toyota isn't there. They still haven't come back from the meeting.

14

Dad's wild. His body is humming with anger. 'Not enough cattle? How the hell can they . . .'

They're flying along the gravel road, through the open country, the long line of flat-topped hills beside them. Dad has been ranting and raving about the Company all the way back from the meeting. Mum keeps shaking her head. *This is the end*, she thinks. *We can't keep this up. We're going to have to go.*

Lofty sits in the front beside Dad, the Company man's voice playing over and over in his mind. 'You need to reduce labour and cut costs,' he'd said looking straight at Lofty. Dad said, 'There's only me and my wife on the place, can't get lower than that. But the bloke kept staring at Lofty, not game to say anything, but making it clear that he wanted Lofty and Red off the place. No one else seemed to notice. They were all arguing among themselves.

As they turn into the house paddock Dad notices the lift of dust in the yards.

'What the bloody hell?'

They're coming. Shane stands up, leaning against the rails, his leg throbbing, throbbing. Red stands in front of him to hide the blood.

'What's going on?' Dad asks through the Toyota window, his voice cold.

'Nothing much,' Shane says. He's trying to be tough but his face is white and clammy. And Roman is running around the yard, white-eyed, the rope trailing out behind him.

'Shane! What's happened?' Mum runs up to him and touches the cut above his eye. 'Give us a look.'

'It's nothing.'

Dad's out of the car, bending through the rails. Lofty grabs a rope and follows.

'Dad! He'll go for you!'

'No he won't.'

'Let me have a look at your leg,' Mum says.

'It's all right. Just a bit of bark off.' Shane pushes her away. 'Dad, don't.'

Dad and Lofty are walking toward Roman. He turns to face them. Dad swings his rope.

'Don't!' Shane screams. 'Mum, I didn't want this to happen!'

'I know, love, but you can't let him win,' Mum says. 'He'll end up a rogue. You'll never be able to trust him. Come and get that leg seen to. You don't want to watch this.'

'No!' Shane says, and then, real quiet, 'It's my fault. I should have waited.'

Roman watches Dad's rope go round and round. He's caught by the stillness and the confidence of the enemy. The slow turn of the loop. Then the rope's floating in a circle toward him.

He tries to duck, but at the same time Lofty sends another loop spinning just above the ground, landing in a circle under the horse's back legs.

Dad's rope drops over Roman's neck. He tries to jump forward to attack Dad, but Lofty's rope tightens on his back legs, locking them together.

Dad twists the rope around his hand, anchors it behind his back and leans down on it, pulling it tight. Roman leaps into the air, twisting, kicking, trying to get away. But every time he lands the ropes get tighter and tighter till he's standing, head down, body dark with sweat, flanks sucked in, nostrils flaring, the whites of his eyes wide in panic.

'Lay him down?' Lofty asks.

'Gonna have to. Won't give in otherwise.'

The two men move apart, stretching the big horse out between them. Roman fights. Kicking, jerking. Even when he can only move a few centimetres he struggles and struggles. He's swaying with exhaustion but he won't fall. His will holds him up.

The ropes stretch him out. The lasso tightens around his throat, cutting off all air. His eyes are bulging, tongue out. A thick rasping sound fills the air as he tries to breathe.

'Dad, don't!' Shane yells, trying to climb through the rails.

'Give in, you mongrel!' Dad growls between clenched teeth. 'Go down!'

And Roman falls.

Shane's through the rails, limping toward the horse.

'Shane, get on him. Lie over him,' Dad says. 'Keep him down.'

'Red!' Lofty calls to Red to take over the hind rope.

Roman tries to kick, to get up, but Shane's on his neck, holding him down. Lofty ties a cloth over the horse's eyes and loosens the rope around his neck to make a halter. The instant the rope loosens, Roman tries to bite, but Lofty twists a loop around his mouth and takes up the slack again, anchoring the horse's head to the ground with his knee.

'Rub him all over,' Dad says, walking out of the yard. 'Don't let him up till he calms down and acknowledges you.'

Shane lies right across the horse. He rubs him behind the ears and over the blindfold. 'It's right, big fella. It's right.'

The horse breathes loudly, his body jerking as he tries to stand. Lofty puts hobbles on his front and back legs, a chain between them, and ties the halter down to the chain. Then him and Red join Dad and Mum where they're sitting on the rails. Red crosses her fingers, her legs, even her toes to give Shane luck in taming the big horse.

Shane rubs his hand over the horse. The salty smell and the heat rising from Roman's sweating body surrounds him. 'It's all right now, big fella. No one is going to hurt you anymore.'

Roman's skin shivers with revulsion as Shane touches him but Shane insists, touching Roman's mouth, holding the softness. The bristles of hair bend under his hands. 'That's it, big fella. C'mon.' He keeps talking. 'You're right,' he says, 'You're right,' over and over.

The sweat on Roman's skin is starting to dry into white patches before he finally stops struggling.

'That's it. No one is going to hurt you again,' Shane says, talking just to let the horse hear his voice. 'We're going to be best mates, you and me.' He whistles three short notes. Roman's ears prick forward to the strange sound.

Shane whistles again and holds his hand over Roman's nose. 'That's me,' he says, tickling the horse's mouth with his fingers. 'When you hear that whistle, it's me.'

At first Roman snorts the smell of Shane away. But finally he relaxes and breathes him in, acknowledging him.

Relief washes through Shane's body. *Yes. Please make him be all right, please.* He rubs Roman all over, leaning on him, rubbing his legs and his rump. He goes back to Roman's head again and again, to put his hand under the horse's nose so Roman has to smell him, and to whisper into the horse's laid-back ears. And then he sits up to whistle the three short notes that will bind them together.

Hours later, those three shorts notes make Roman's ears lift to hear, inquiring. And the next time Shane puts his hand over Roman's mouth, the horse lifts his lips to touch the hand, tasting, smelling.

Shane looks up at Red, nearly crying with joy. He has to swallow hard to disperse the hard lump in his throat before he can call out to say, 'He's right, Dad. Let him up?'

Dad nods, and Shane steps off the horse, lifting the halter.

Roman bounces up, snorts, and jerks his head up so that it jolts against the chain tied down to the hobbles. He's blind-folded. He can't see. His legs are tied together. Panic rises in his chest. *What's going on?*

Shane whistles to him again. 'It's all right, mate. Calm down. Everything's all right.' And his now-familiar voice and smell settles the horse. 'Red, can ya bring us a bucket of water?'.

· · ·

'Got you a drink, mate. Here.' Shane's talking to Roman all the time so the horse knows exactly where he is. He brings the water close so Roman can smell it. The horse's nostrils flare.

'Here. Here.' Shane encourages him by pulling on the halter.

And with aching steps Roman moves closer to Shane and finally gulp, gulps the cool water while Shane's hands soothe his aching neck, his shoulders.

'Can I take the blindfold and hobbles off?'

Dad shakes his head. 'Not too fast. One wrong move and you're back to square one. Bring Chocolate in and leave him for a couple of hours.'

'Come and get that leg fixed now,' Mum says.

'It's right, Mum.'

'Shane.'

'Leave the kid alone,' Dad says. He puts his arm around Mum, 'Come on,' and they drive back up to the big house.

Shane puts some hay under Roman's nose and rubs his face again. 'Sorry, mate,' he whispers into the horse's ears. 'I should have waited.'

Red brings Chocolate over and she leans against Roman. He nuzzles her.

Shane feels suddenly weak; his skin clammy and cold, a huge lump expands in his chest, his guts feel empty. The world's swaying.

'What's the matter?' Red grabs him.

He leans against her, shaking his head. 'Don't know. I can't see properly.'

'Grandad?' he hears her yell to Lofty.

Then nothing.

15

———

Shane's soaking in the bath, his whole body stinging. He's naked. *Naked?* 'Hey!' He quickly covers himself with his hands. *Mum!* Guilt and shame wash through his body. Mum's talking, reckons he fainted. Red and Lofty had to carry him up to the house. Delayed shock. Had to cut his jeans off. 'Sorry,' she goes back to squirting salty water into the wounds on his leg to flush the dirt out. 'Sorry mate. But you don't want an infection. I know it hurts. Sorry.'

'Mum, shuddup. Just do it.' His eyes are closed, the pain screaming through his brain.

She's silent then, scrubbing, frowning to stop her voice.

And then he's alone, the water soothing his aching muscles. He can hear Lofty and Dad in the lounge room, talking about the meeting.

'Had to get out of there before I punched someone,' Dad says. 'The Company prides itself on producing top quality in trying economic times. We're in seventy countries throughout the known world.' Dad imitates the American businessman.

Red laughs.

Red! Did she see me naked?

The inter-station radio beeps and Mum answers it. 'Turkey Flat, over,' her voice is light, still laughing at Dad's imitation of an American accent.

It's Geraldine from Dry River. Everyone's still talking and laughing in the background.

'What?'

Suddenly they're all quiet and Mum's turned the radio up. Geraldine's voice crackles a little, loud and very serious. She's talking about the meeting, saying what happened after Dad's mob stormed out.

'Downsize.' Shane strains to hear what she's saying. 'Combine Goose Creek, Dry River and Turkey Flat to make one big station. One manager. Less administration. Bring in labour as it's needed. We've all got to apply for the manager's job. Everyone else has to go.'

'They can get stuffed!' Dad yells out.

'Bill!' Mum says.

'No bull! I'm not fighting with people we've known for years for their poxy little job. They can get stuffed.'

Shane climbs out of the bath, his legs shaking. *No way! They can't kick us off. This is our land. Our family's been here forever.* He leans into the doorframe, a towel around his waist.

Dad's standing, his finger still pointing at the radio. Red's sitting, stunned. Lofty slowly gets to his feet, lifting his hands to ask Mum, *What about us?*

'Geraldine? Lofty and his granddaughter? Can they stay?'

Silence. Then, 'Is he there?' Geraldine whispers.

'Yeah.' Mum's voice is tentative.

'We're all here, Geraldine,' Dad says. 'Get it off ya chest.'

'He was very specific about Lofty. He wants them off the

property straight away. Reckons they should have gone long ago. That by rights they're trespassing.'

'Trespass? What-you-mean, trespass,' Lofty yells to Dad. 'This my country.'

'Mongrel dogs!' Dad says.

Lofty storms toward the radio, 'This my country!'

Dad steps forward, worried that Lofty might smash the radio in his anger.

'I've got this country.' Lofty spins around to him.

'Yeah, but they own it.'

They face each other.

'Why? Geraldine, why? He's never done any harm,' Mum's saying.

'They've been worried about Lofty ever since the Mabo court decision. They reckon if some Aboriginal people can fight to get their land back, others might be encouraged to try as well,' Geraldine replies softly.

'But Lofty would never—'

'Well, perhaps he should,' Geraldine interrupts. 'He has every right to fight for his land.'

Silence.

Mum doesn't know what to say. Geraldine's a bit of a do-gooder when it comes to Aboriginal people. She's never lived with them. She and her family didn't even come up to the north till after 'equal pay', when all the Aboriginal workers got hunted off the stations. But that doesn't stop her being full of good ideas.

Silence.

Then Mum says, 'Thanks Geraldine. Talk to you later.'

· · ·

Lofty's walking up and down, his body stiff with anger. 'This my country. Properly. They can't kick me. I got land right.'

'Lofty, your land rights don't count. The Company bought this land fair and square.'

'They stole this country!'

Dad and Lofty look hard at each other. If this land was stolen, then it was Dad's great-grandfather who stole it. Dad and Lofty have lived together since Dad was born and have never talked about this.

The room is filled with tension. Spoken words could destroy their fifty-year-long friendship so they keep their mouths closed, only their eyes speak, dark with anger.

'Can you prove this is your country, Lofty?' Mum asks, trying to mediate.

'What-you-mean prove. This my country.'

'If you try to get land rights, they'll fight you through the court.'

'I'll get that land right mob. I got all the stories. I got everything for this country.'

'They got the title. They paid for it. They own it,' Mum says. 'You're just like us. Once we owned this land too, but we lost it, Lofty. It's all ancient history.'

'Yeah, but if the land was stolen, then the Company could be had up for accepting stolen goods,' Shane says.

Mum and Dad spin round on him, their faces furious. He pulls a face and lifts his hands to say, *Just a joke.*

'I'd keep my mouth shut if I was you,' Dad says.

Shane limps to the lounge room and holding his towel tight between his legs, sits down, lifting his sore leg up onto the coffee table. Mum grabs a box of dressings and starts fixing his cut face and his burned fingers, and putting ointment and gauze over the wounds on his legs. The only sound in the room is the *rip, rip* as she tears up an old sheet into bandages.

Lofty's crumpled in a chair. *They can't make me leave. This my land. Where we gonna go? A camp outside a town somewhere?*

Dad's brain is swollen with anger.

'Isn't Geraldine's son a land rights lawyer?' Shane says. 'We can ask him. See if Lofty could get land rights. If he gets land rights then we could all stay here.' He looks at Lofty for confirmation.

Dad snorts with disgust. Shane doesn't look at him. 'Mum?'

She stares at him. Their eyes lock in silent argument. *We've got to help them. Lofty will die if he has to leave his country.*

We might not agree with the Company but it's their land. How would you feel if it was your land and someone was trying to take it?

What about Red? What's going to happen to Red?

Mum looks away.

'Me and Red are doing land rights for our assignment,' Shane says. 'You know that independent research assignment we have to do? We're doing land rights, so we have to talk to a lawyer anyway.'

Mum looks back at him. 'First I heard about this,' she says.

'The other day we started it, when youse were mustering,' he says, holding his face real honest.

'*You* mob not youse,' she corrects his English.

'When you mob were mustering. Hey Red? But we couldn't get enough information. So what we thought was, that we could interview people around here. Tell them, Red! Didn't we?'

This is the first Red's heard about any land rights assignment. But she nods and, thinking quickly, says, 'You know how you always reckon you got to be balanced in essays? We thought that if we could interview all the local people, Auntie Clara and all that Bunuba mob in town, and the malngarri that been here for a long time, and find out about the law stuff, it'd be a really good essay.'

'Well, you know my thoughts on land rights,' Dad says, trying to stop the conversation.

'Yeah, but we'd need to interview you to get your exact words,' Red says, gammon real earnest. 'That way we can put forward all the sides of the story.'

Dad leans back in his chair, shaking his head in disbelief.

'Mum?' Shane asks.

Mum turns and looks at Shane, her face stiff. 'Well, I can tell you how this place was first settled,' she says. 'How hard it was for the first settlers. How many of their children died.'

Shane concentrates hard on keeping his face open and honest, pretending to meet her eye but looking at the air between them to stop her seeing right through him.

'So can we do the assignment then?' he forces himself to say. 'Can I ring Geraldine and get her son's number?'

The lounge room is quiet. Dad and Lofty are staring at the floor.

'Don't you think we should pass it by Miss Mandy first?' Mum says, lifting her eyebrows. 'I'm sure she'd like to have some input into the type of topic you choose.'

'I'll ring her.' Red jumps up and runs into the kitchen to the telephone.

Please be there. Please be there, Shane thinks as he hobbles in after her.

'Don't tell her too much, she always talks to Mum,' he whispers.

'I'm not stupid.'

Miss Mandy is there. Red tells her about the assignment, then listens and looks at Shane, nodding. 'Yes, we've got a tape recorder,' she says.

'Ask her about the law,' Shane interrupts.

She lifts her finger to tell him to wait, listens, and then says, 'Yeah. See ya,' and hangs up.

'I told you to . . .' Shane says.

'She's sending research books on the mail plane,' Red says. 'We'll get that law stuff from Geraldine's son.'

16

―――――

Back in the lounge room, Red tells the others.

'Miss Mandy said no worries. Reckons it'd make an excellent assignment. She's gonna send some stuff out on the mail plane tomorrow.'

'So can we ring Geraldine to get her son's number?' Shane says.

Silence.

Dad stands up and starts walking out of the room. 'Shane, come with me,' he says, his voice cold.

Shane follows him out. *Oh-oh. Big trouble.* They get in the bull-catcher and start driving.

'The Company bought this land fair and square.'

'But what about us? It's our land too. And they're kicking us off.'

'It's not our land. We sold it.'

'Our family's been here forever. You were born here. I was born here. My grandfather was even born here.'

Dad stops at the yards and turns to Shane. 'You reckon I don't feel wild? You reckon I like this? Sometimes things happen that you can't change. The sooner you learn that the better. We'll be right. We'll start again.'

Roman's standing nibbling at the hay, blindfolded and hobbled, but calm.

Dad goes on. 'Land rights are wrong. Lofty's just angry. He'll come around. He's always been a good bloke. Always worked – never been a bludger. He wouldn't . . .'

Shane stops listening. The words blend together. Then there's silence.

Dad's looking at Roman. 'Better take the blindfold off that horse,' he says, getting out of the bull-catcher.

'Dad, can I? It's just . . .'

'I know. You want to work him yourself, so he's a one-man horse. But you won't be able to move fast enough with that leg. What if he goes for you?'

'I'll be careful.' Shane says, and crawls through the rails.

'Talk to him so he knows where you are.'

Shane whistles softly, three short notes. Roman pricks his ears, lifts his head. Chocolate ignores the whistle. It's not hers.

'That's the way.' Shane whistles again. 'Stand up. Let's take that blindfold off and have a look at you, hey?' He's limping toward the horses, his voice low and firm, trying to sound confident.

Roman snorts and tries to step back. The hobbles jerk against his legs. He panics, lifting both front legs together, bouncing from side to side. He shakes his head, trying to get the blindfold off.

'Steady!' Dad yells from the rails. 'Be careful!'

Shane stops. 'Stand up, you right. Stand up.' He talks to the horse so Roman knows he's not coming any closer. The big horse is still, his skin trembling.

'You right. You right.' Shane inches forward again, stopping each time Roman moves, waiting and talking to him till he's calm again.

Waiting. Then moving forward again, his hand outstretched. Until finally his hand's right there.

And Roman lifts his nose to smell the hand, snorts and pulls back.

'Nah, nah. C'mon. You right.'

He lifts his nose again, to sniff. He opens his lips to touch Shane's hand.

And then Shane's running his hand up Roman's face and around his ears behind the blindfold. The big horse nudges him.

Dad shakes his head, breathes a thin whistle out through pursed lips. *That's good. Real good,* he thinks.

Shane smiles, unable to believe it himself. He undoes the knot and loosens the blindfold. 'It's all right. Everything's all right. Might come as a shock how ugly I am but I'm not going to hurt you.' He keeps talking, saying any kind of nonsense that comes into his head, trying to keep the horse calm.

Light! People! Roman snorts and backs away. Shane slowly reaches out his hand. 'C'mon Roman. Big man.'

And Roman looks at him right in the eyes like an equal, his front legs firm in the soil.

'That's it. C'mon.' Shane's outstretched hand hangs in the air between them. An offering.

Roman lowers his face and gives the soft warmth of his breath to Shane's palm, tasting the smell of him, breathing him in.

Shane whistles the three short notes. Roman's ears spring forward, enquiring. He sniffs Shane's face with his nose. It's soft and sharp, like velvet with prickles.

'Doing good,' Dad says, loud enough for Shane to hear, so proud his throat's all tight. 'Real good.'

Shane's face is glowing with pride.

There are footsteps. It's Lofty. Shane smiles at Dad to say, *Lofty is going to see how I've got Roman working already. He's going to be impressed, hey?*

But Dad's face is hard as stone. He closes his eyes to say, *Just leave it!*

Lofty leans into the rails and starts talking to the horse in Language. 'You ready old man?' he asks. 'You ready to meet this boy?'

The big horse turns one ear sideways to listen, lifts his head and calls out to Lofty in a long neigh, nodding his head up and down. Then he nudges Shane again, shoving his head right under Shane's armpit, pushing against him.

Lofty smiles. 'You're a good horseman, Shane,' he says.

Shane grins and puts his head down embarrassed, not wanting to look too proud.

'Give you hand with that fence,' Lofty says to Dad in English.

Silence. Dad's just standing there, ignoring Lofty, his eyes on the horse. For ages.

Dad?

Finally he says, 'You're all right. I'll fix it later.' But he doesn't look at Lofty. He keeps his back to him like he doesn't know him. Like they haven't been friends since Dad was born. As if it wasn't Lofty who taught him how to ride a horse or to dog a micky bull, or how to travel through deep shadows in the stone country to find the cattle hidden there.

'Dad?'

Dad looks at Shane, cold. His eyes say, *You got something you want to say? You the one started this land right business.*

Shane looks away. They hear Lofty leave.

Then Dad says, 'Bag him down good before you take them hobbles off,' and goes too.

Shane nods. He hears the bull-catcher start and Dad drive round to the shed, and then down to the bottom paddock to fix the fence by himself. Shane rubs Roman's neck with the blindfold, slow and steady, moving it down along his back. 'There, you see. Feel that. Good, hey?' He's talking as much to disperse the fear lifting his guts as to quieten the horse. He has never known Dad and Lofty to fight before. They have never even had an argument.

'Your mum said put the house cow away,' Red yells as she runs past.

'Red!'

She turns and laughs back at him, 'Wait. Gotta tell Lofty something,' and goes.

'She'll be back,' Shane tells Roman. 'She'll want to see how you're working. Won't be able to help herself.'

But she doesn't come back. *Must've got hold of Geraldine's son and she's telling him all the goss.*

Clouds build up white and thin across the sky. It's hot. Stinking hot. Roman's chest is dark with sweat. He stands stiffly while Shane brushes him down the neck, across the chest and around his ears.

When the late afternoon sun turns the clouds red, Roman's hobbles come off. Shane's puts a halter on him and starts rubbing him all over with a blanket. Still Red doesn't come back. Shane's heart sinks. Lofty must've told her that Dad ignored him.

Should go over there to say ... What? What can you say?

Roman nudges his hand, but Shane's distracted, thinking about Lofty and Dad. I know, he thinks, I'll just gammon start walking back home. Red will see me and yell out, and then I can go and talk to them. Explain to them.

He finishes rubbing Roman down quickly and walks up the path toward the big house.

But Red doesn't yell out. No one does.

Shane's too embarrassed to look in at Lofty's place, to see if they're there, because what if they are there and they just turn their heads away from him? So he walks straight past, his silhouette black against the blood-red sky.

17

Next day Dad is real quiet. He has his morning coffee on the veranda with Mum, instead of down at the yards with Lofty where they'd normally talk the day over.

Shane stays inside the house. *Why did I start this land rights stuff?* His guts are empty with worry. *I bet Red doesn't even come up for school.*

But she does, and Shane runs out to meet her. 'Red, thought you wouldn't come.'

'Why?'

'It's just . . .'

'What?'

Then Lofty is walking up the path and up the steps. 'Morning missus,' he says to Mum, as if nothing's wrong, and sits down at the outside table with Dad.

'Want some breakfast?' Mum says. She's so glad to see him and desperate for everything to be all right.

'Fencing today?' Lofty asks Dad.

Dad shrugs his shoulders.

Shane's just inside the door, listening. He feels sick. Dad

is still seething with anger. What if he starts yelling at Lofty, telling him to bugger off?

Red goes into the schoolroom, gets her books out and sits down at the desk. Shane follows her in. She says, 'We gotta ring Geraldine and get her son's number.'

'I don't know if . . .' Shane says.

She turns on him. 'What?'

He points with his lips to Dad.

'We gotta get this land, Shane,' Red whispers, her head forward, staring into his eyes.

He looks away. 'Just wait till he goes.'

They wait. And wait. Doodling on their pads. Pretending to work on their maths assignment. But Dad and Lofty just keep sitting out there. Shane and Red hear Lofty say something, then silence, then Dad's monosyllabic response. Then there's a long silence. Another bit of quiet talk and another long silence.

They wait. And wait. And wait. Mum comes in to sort out next week's work.

'I can't stand this,' Red gets up and walks over to Mum. 'Can we ring Geraldine and get her son's number?' she whispers.

Mum looks out at Dad, nods, and puts her finger up to her lips to say, *Keep it quiet.*

Shane runs into the kitchen.

'Let me phone.' Red rushes past, real pushy.

And when she gets through to Geraldine's son, Neil, she is gammon real efficient explaining about Lofty: how they're going to be kicked off their land and how they want to try for land rights.

'Yeah, Mum said you might ring,' Neil says. 'But there's no

land rights in Western Australia. Only in the Northern Territory. You are going to have to try for native title,' he says. 'Did you hear about Mabo?' And he starts raving on about the Mabo High Court case, the 'Wik Decision' and the '10-Point Plan' and 'unbroken tenure' and 'proof of ownership' and 'negotiation'.

Red tries to make notes but she can't write and listen at the same time.

'Here, let me,' Shane says, grabbing the paper. 'Tell me what to write.'

Red rolls her eyes, *you can't write quickly.*

Just give it to me.

In the end, 'Look, to be honest,' Neil tells Red, 'you haven't got much of a chance of getting the station. But if you can prove that Lofty comes from that country and that he still exercises traditional customs on the land – like hunting and ceremonies – then he might get access.'

Dad's sitting outside trying to keep his anger alive, but Lofty is just chatting about the station, what work needs to be done, as if nothing's happened. As if they're staying. Dad can feel his anger softening and it annoys him. He gets up, 'I'll make a cuppa,' he says.

Neil's still talking on the phone. 'A lot of the time station people took kids from other places because the kids couldn't run away if their family lived hundreds of miles away. Lofty could be from anywhere.'

'Nah, he definitely comes from here,' Red says.

Dad walks in. Shane holds his breath. His body's suddenly light with fear. *Did Dad hear what Red just said?*

Dad grabs the jug right next to them and fills it up. Neil keeps talking in Red's ear but her heart is thumping so loudly she can't hear him.

Dad turns the notebook around and looks at Shane's notes.

What have I written? How will he react?

'How the hell can you read that scribble, Shane?' Dad asks. He moves away to put tea in the teapot, clunks the cups, milk and sugar onto the tray, taking forever.

'Yep. Yep,' Red whispers, taking the pen from Shane and scribbling notes.

Finally the tea is made, and Dad picks up the tray and walks out.

'I'll ring Mum and find a number for this Company bloke,' Neil's saying, 'and make sure he understands his obligations under the Native Title Act. That'll keep them off your back in the short term. I'll ring back when I've talked to them. Meantime, see what you can find out and we'll talk later.'

Red puts down the phone, and she and Shane look at the notes. 'Grandad did come from here,' she says. 'And he's got all the ceremonies.' She looks at Shane and laughs, punching him on the arm. 'It's gonna be right. We're gonna stay!'

They hear a light plane in the distance. Red looks at the clock. 'The mail plane. The books!'

Dad dumps the mailbag on the table and leaves.

Red tips it upside down so everything falls out. 'Here.' She grabs the box of books, runs to the schoolroom and rips it open.

Jandamarra? There's a book about Jandamarra! They can't have a book about Jandamarra. How can malngarri know about that? She holds it tight to her chest. Shane reaches out his hand to have a look at the book but she ignores him, wrapping her arms tighter around it, and walks out to the veranda, where Lofty is still sitting with Dad.

She stares at Lofty.

Lofty looks at her. *What's the matter?*

'This book's about Jandamarra,' she tells him in Language.

'Aih? They can't do that.'

Dad sits up, listening. Dad sits up, listening. He grew up speaking Language with Lofty so understands what they are saying. Red reads the author's name on the cover.

'Whatkind?' Lofty says. 'Bunuba people writing books now?'

'It's a malngarri story too,' Dad snaps.

'Give me look.' Lofty takes the book and turns the pages. 'Aih, poor thing!' There's pictures of black people with chains around their necks. He touches the photographs, stroking the people.

Silence. A long shameful silence.

'Lot of writing. Who can read it?' Lofty asks Dad.

'Anyone. Once that story is in a book anyone who can read can know that story.'

Lofty's face is horrified. He can't read English but he wants to know what the book says. To see if they got the proper story. To see if it is the whole story, the sacred parts too. He hands it to Dad. 'You read it,' he says.

'I haven't got time—'

'I nomore subbie didjun,' Lofty says in heavy Kriol. *You know I can't read English.*

Dad looks at Mum, pressuring her to read it.

'No. You read it,' Lofty says in Language. 'They might have the whole story in here.' Lofty holds Dad's eyes with his own.

Women and kids can't read this, he's saying. *This is men's business.*

'All right.' Dad puts his hand out to take the book, takes his glasses off the table and, sitting with his back stiff and uncomfortable in his chair, he starts reading.

He reads one page, two pages, skimming over the words. Lofty sits on the edge of his chair watching, waiting, listening to Dad read.

Then Dad stops. 'Lofty, it's gonna take a long time, one day or two. We can't just sit around all day reading books.' He starts to stand up.

''S'all right,' Lofty says, lifting his hand to say, *Stay there.* 'I'll do the fence. When I come back d'rectly you give me that story.'

Dad rolls his eyes and sits down again to read.

When Lofty comes back at dinnertime he sits again on the veranda and Dad tells him what he's read so far about how Jandamarra killed the policeman Richardson and hid in the hills. 'That book reckons they hunted him. The malngarri hunted him.' He stops, unable to say, *And they killed all the people on the land.*

'Yeah, that's right. That's the right one.' Lofty nods, lifting his hand to say, *And?*

Dad coughs to clear his throat, denial clouding his brain. *I know they were tough on the Aboriginal people, those early settlers,* he's thinking. *I know a lot of people got killed. But the malngarri were fighting for their lives too. The way Grandad told it, it was Grandad running scared, not . . .*

Lofty doesn't notice Dad's discomfort. His relationship with Dad's family has always incorporated this knowledge.

And like accepted knowledge, he thinks that everyone has it, that everyone knows.

The phone rings inside. Dad jumps up to answer it. Anything to get away from Lofty's questions.

Shane and Red run out of the schoolroom. *Maybe it's Neil. Dad?* They meet him in the doorway and try to rush past.

'I'll get it,' Dad says, and picks up the phone. 'Turkey Flat.' He listens. 'Yes?' His face is surprised. It's someone he doesn't know.

It's Neil.

'What?' Dad yells, wild.

Shane and Red turn to sneak out the door. There's going to be big trouble.

'You can't do that!' Dad yells.

They stop. *Is he talking to us?*

'You can get stuffed!' Dad slams down the phone.

Mum comes in, lifting her eyebrows to ask what's happening. Dad's leaning back against the bench.

'They've given us a week to get off the place.'

18

————————

'No!' Shane yells. 'No way. We're not leaving. Dad, we rang about the land rights. They reckon Lofty's got a chance.'

'You what?' Dad says.

What's going on? Lofty asks at the door with a twist of his hand.

'They're kicking us off,' Red says. 'But we're going for land rights.'

Dad tries to say something, but Shane interrupts him. 'Dad, it's our only chance.'

'Shane,' Dad threatens.

'No, it's true,' Red says. 'That bloke reckons they can't kick us off if we can – where is it?' She reads from the notes: 'Prove that native title hasn't been stuffed up.'

'Yeah. They can't hunt me. This my country,' Lofty says.

'It's been a pastoral lease for more than a hundred years,' Dad says.

'Neil reckons it doesn't matter. If we've still got that' – Red looks again at the notes and can't read Shane's writing, so makes it up – 'if people still hunt and do ceremony on the land, they still got native title. Hey Shane?'

'Leave it!' Dad yells.

Shane stares at Dad. 'No. I'm not leaving it,' he says, his eyes shining with tears. 'I'm not leaving this place. I'll go bush and ambush them. Steal their cattle.'

'Shane!' Mum's shocked.

'Whose cattle you going to steal, Shane?' Dad says. 'Geraldine and Steve's, if they get the job? Are you going to make their life hard? Get them the sack?'

Shane can't talk. His throat's thick with anger, his brain boiling in turmoil, his face stiff trying not to cry and lose his temper or scream at his father. Dad's eyes, narrow and dark, are staring him down, but Shane looks right back, drilling in with his thoughts: *I don't care what you say, I'm staying. I'm fighting to the death.*

'Perhaps we should find out more about this Land Rights thing for Lofty and Red's sake,' Mum says.

'What?' said Dad.

'Well, you got any better ideas?' Mum asks him, her eyes sparkling.

Lofty gets up and stands next to Mum. Dad keeps looking at her. *You're turning on me now, on everything you believe in, our history. Everything we are. Don't do it.*

'We got nowhere else to go,' Red says to Dad, and walks over to stand with Mum.

They're all together, Shane, Lofty, Red and Mum. Dad looks from one to the other, shaking his head with disbelief.

'What have we got to lose?' Mum says to him, her voice softer.

Silence.

Shane follows her eyes. Dad's face is crushed, defeated.

'Dad?'

Dad doesn't look up. He just grabs his hat and walks out. The dogs see him come down the steps and run over to meet him, bouncing up to lick his hands, lifting the dust around his boots. 'Get out!' he yells at them.

They duck and slink behind him to follow at a safe distance.

Shane hobbles out onto the veranda and watches his father walk away, the image unfocused with tears. Dad's upset. Not wild. Not angry or belligerent but . . . different. Sad. Defeated. Shane's suddenly frightened. Frightened for his dad as well as himself. *Got to make him understand.*

Dad steps into the bull-catcher and it purrs down to the yards. Shane pulls on his boots and follows. But when he gets closer, he doesn't know what to do. Dad's sitting there in the bull-catcher, bent over the steering wheel. His shoulders are moving, jerking. No way! *Is he crying?*

Shane stops, embarrassed. He wants to run back to the house but he stays, turning his head away so he can't see.

We're buggered. Four generations we been here, Dad's thinking, looking out over the stockyards at the hazy purple hills in the distance. *I was born looking at this country. What'll it be like to be banished forever? To never see that view again?*

Roman is walking around the yard. 'Weakness,' Dad says to the big horse. 'That's what it's all about. Your enemies will always prey on your weaknesses. For Pigeon it was his mother and his people. For you, big horse, it's the mares. Me? I've given away my pride to live here where I was born, on the country I know and love. They know I'll do anything to stay, so they treat me like a dog.'

Then Shane is right there at his elbow. 'Dad?'

Dad coughs. 'Better get a saddle on that horse,' he says, his voice croaky.

'Dad, that bloke Neil reckons we can apply for access. We don't have to take the land back. We can just stay here, like, have access.'

'Shane, that horse needs seeing to.'

Back at the house, Mum says, 'So do you still do ceremonies, Lofty?'

'I got that story. I've got everything for this country,' Lofty says.

'You'll have to tell the court all that secret business,' she says. 'Tell them malngarri everything. Would you do that?'

'I can say that one. That story belongs to me. I can speak all those stories.'

'But Neil reckons you can't do ceremony by yourself,' Red says. 'He reckons that court won't believe just one old man has been keeping up the ceremony on this place.'

'I got that ceremony,' Lofty says, getting angry. 'I got that story, I got everything.' He's annoyed he has to talk about these things to women and kids.

'All right,' Mum says. 'Now, how can we get proof your family comes from here?'

'We are here,' Lofty says. 'This my father's country. All them old people still here, buried here' he says, spreading his arms to encompass the floodplain, the stone country, right around. 'From my father, grandfather, great-grandfather, all the way. Ask anyone. They know.'

'We need more malngarri kind of proof. Do you have paintings or middens? Or what? How can we prove it? So that the judge can see.' Suddenly Mum stands up. 'Station diaries!'

Lofty and Red look at her.

'They recorded all the births at the station camp. We did too, till everyone left. Come on, Red, give us a hand,' Mum says, and she races out to get the ladder.

Mum and Red are in the ceiling, scratching and shuffling as they move along the beams. 'Here they are.' There's the sound of something heavy being dragged.

'Keep it on the beams or we'll go straight through.'

Drag, drag, thump, thump. And they're coming down the ladder, Mum carrying a big box. A big black strongbox with curved-over edges, old-fashioned, with a flat lock, dust and spiderwebs clinging to the corners. *That's the box now from the old station time,* Lofty thinks. *That's the box that measured every-one. Shane's great-grandfather kept the tobacco and a bit of money in that box. It held his power, all his potency and knowledge. You had to give your life and pride for what that box held.*

He was a hard man, that old man, Lofty remembers. *Hard on Shane's grandfather too. That many floggings we got, both of us – with a stock-whip too. But then Shane's grandfather went away droving. Stayed away for years. He didn't have to stay and prove himself to the old man, time and time again. He only came back when the old man was tired and ready to let him take over the station.* Lofty turns his face away. A long time ago, he had decided it was better to do without what that box had to offer. But now . . .

Mum unlocks the box and pulls out the station diaries. Two old books, leather bound. She opens one, flicks through the pages. The smell of stillness and age lifts from the paper and surrounds them. The pages are soft and yellowing with lines of beautiful curved writing, ink pen, thin, then thick.

They huddle together watching as she turns the pages. 'There! Ambrose,' she says.

'Ambrose?' Red laughs. 'Is that what they called you, Grandad?'

Lofty looks hard at her and she pulls her lips down to stop the smile.

'Doreen. That's your mother, hey Lofty?' Mum says.

Lofty looks. 'Where?'

Red shows him the name. Next to it is written, *1934 male son, Ambrose.*

Lofty's eyes hold the word. He touches it, *Doreen,* his finger black against the cream paper.

'We just have to trace her right back,' Mum says, flicking back through the pages. 'Look, here she is, born to the house girl Doris in 1918.' Mum's flicking more pages. 'Doris was born in 1902. That's it, that's as far as it goes. That old man moved onto the place in 1900 when he was eighteen.'

'Reckon that's enough?'

'Yep.'

'Where am I?' Red asks, scraping the chair as she pulls it up to the table, looking to find herself in the more modern book. 'There's Grandad and Auntie Clara, Uncle Conway. But I'm not here, or Shane. Where's me and Shane?'

Lofty looks at Mum. Mum looks away. Red's questions hang in the air between them. For a long time the births of Bunuba children on stations, like calves and foals, were recorded in the station book. Their date of birth, sex, any outstanding characteristics.

Red looks up at Mum, *Why aren't you answering?*

'That was an old custom,' Mum says, trying to change the subject.

'When was Shane's dad born?'

'He won't be there either.'

'Why?'

'Red, ring Neil back and tell him we've got proof,' Mum says,

'Is it just Bunuba people they wrote down in the book?'

Mum lifts her eyebrows. 'Will you ring, or will I?'

Red goes.

'That's brilliant,' Neil says when she tells him. 'Brilliant.'

'So you reckon that's enough?'

'Too right. Can't argue with official station documentation,' Neil says. But Red doesn't get his joke, so he continues. 'There are a number of Sacred Sites registered in the stone country there. That land's useless to the station. So I'll ask them to negotiate over the stone country. We might even get title to it if we let Native Title slip on the station. That's all negotiable. The main thing is, we got them talking.'

'No access to the good cattle country?' Red says.

'Nothing. They don't even want you driving through. They're worried about people burning the country and shooting cattle.'

'But—'

'Red. You should be happy. This is the quickest result in the world. The hardest part is over. Usually it takes years just to get them talking. Listen, just speak to Lofty and get back to me?'

'Yep.' She puts the phone down. *Bugga.* She walks back into the lounge room, her shoulders slumped.

'What did he say?' Mum asks.

'He reckons they'll only negotiate over the rubbish country.'

'Rubbish?' Lofty asks.

'All that stone country, Dead Man's Peak, Rochter's Pass and that. They won't let us have none of them station paddocks.'

'Nah, nah. That's the one now,' Lofty says standing up. 'Too right. That's the good one. This the rubbish country here now, only good for cattle.'

Mum starts to laugh. 'The way you mob talk. No wonder no one can understand you. Rubbish is what you throw in the bin. It's not country.'

'You tell him,' Lofty insists, pointing and guiding Red back to the phone.

'You want the stone country?'

'That's the one now.'

19

Back in the round yard, Shane's smiling. He's got the saddle blanket over Roman. He's ready to lift the saddle up onto his back when suddenly Roman jerks his head into the air and jumps back.

Shane twists and his leg collapses. He's on the ground, covering his head, in case Roman attacks him again. But the horse stands still, looking past him, ears forward, head high, neck arched.

'What? What is it?' Shane gets up, stretching up on tiptoe to see over the fence.

Dad climbs the stockyard rails and, arms out for balance, stands on the top one, looking out. The hills are purple in the distance, a heat haze shimmers over the paddocks. *Hey! There's some animals down there on the floodplain.* 'The mares,' he says to Shane. 'The mares. They're in the bottom paddock.' He jumps down, and for a moment doesn't know which way to go. 'Come on. Let's go.'

He runs to the bull-catcher, Shane close behind him. The dogs pile in.

'Get back to the house!' Dad yells at them.

They leap out again, no hesitation, and bolt back up to the house.

'There was a time when you were that obedient,' Dad says to Shane.

Shane looks at him and they smile. Then they're off, flat out past the homestead, heading toward the stone country, going around the long way to the bottom paddock, dust spinning up behind them.

This is our chance, Dad's thinking. *If we can get those mares, we've got a chance to stay in this country, to have a life. They're the beginning of a stud herd.* His fingers are crossed on the steering wheel, his body tense, the accelerator flat to the floor.

Past the bottom fenceline, around the corner, back tyres sliding in the sand and there they are, the horses, in the distance.

They're about a hundred metres from the cocky gate. This side's all right, there's fence behind us. If they come this way, we can turn them. But that fence is still broken thirty metres down from where they are. Need to get them up farther or we'll lose them.

Dad turns sharp left and around, coming up toward the horses from behind. They're feeding in a group, nervous, lifting their heads to check for danger. There's a big horse, blood red, with them. It throws its head up and calls. They're all alert, watching.

The big red horse breaks from the herd. Dad hits the horn and turns the bull-catcher around to cut it off. It's a mare, a big brood mare. She hits the skids, sitting down and spinning around in one movement.

Wow.

She trots back to the herd, head high, long mane lifting and floating in the air behind her. Once she's back with the herd she lifts her head to sing out a challenge. Roman answers from up at the yards and she turns toward him, calling again.

Get them moving. Don't give them time to think. Dad moves the bull-catcher toward the horses again.

And they turn and trot toward the yards, tails high, heads up, looking behind, the foal somewhere safe in the middle.

Yes! C'mon, c'mon! Keep going! Keep going! Shane begs.

And they do.

Dad stays back and the horses trot along in a jittery nervous group. Until they see the cocky gate.

Almost there. Come on go through!

But the big red mare props, and the others huddle around her. Dad beeps the horn to keep them moving. The mare turns to face the bull-catcher, front legs apart, crouched, ready to jump.

Dad gets closer.

Her front legs bounce from side to side. Her eyes are wide. And she breaks again. In three jumps she's at a flat gallop, bolting out to the left. Dad spins the wheel, foot to the floor, racing to cut her off. Her head's down, legs stretching, trying to get past.

'Look out, you'll hit her!'

And she jumps. Hoofs fly above their heads.

Duck! Dad screeches on the brakes.

She goes straight over the top of the bull-catcher and she's gone, bolting for the hills.

The others are running too. Dad hits the horn hard, slams down the accelerator, turns the bull-catcher into a 360, spinning up a cloud of dust. He gets in front of them, turning them back.

They're running toward the cocky gate, and they're almost through it when a loud whinny comes from behind them.

That bloody big mare's calling them.

The herd splits. As if they've been given clear instructions, they break into two groups, turn, and gallop flat out on either side of the bull-catcher. Dad rushes to cut off the smaller group, horn blaring. Three mares, two yearlings and the foal. They baulk. The mother with the foal isn't game to take on the bull-catcher, and the others slow down to stay with them. They turn.

This time Dad doesn't give them a moment to think. He rushes at them, beeping the horn all the time, keeping the bull-catcher right on their heels. They rush through the cocky gate and into the spelling yard.

Shane can't even get his foot out the door before Dad's out, pulling the gate closed, his fingers shaking with excitement. He turns his hands into fists and punches the air.

Roman calls out from the stockyards. His voice is loud and urgent. The mares answer and start trotting up to him. He calls again, talking to them, soothing them.

Dad's laughing as he walks back to the bull-catcher. 'This is our chance! Can you believe it? With Roman and these mares, we've got a stud herd!' He steps up on the running board. 'We can get a bit of country and—'

'Dad, what about . . .' Shane points with his thumb up at the stone country.

'Can't make a living up there, mate. There's no feed. We'll get one of them small blocks. A couple of thousand acres outside Timber Creek or Halls Creek.'

'There must be feed. Roman's lived up there for years,' Shane says.

'Shane. I'm not living on handouts. Lofty's got his pension, but what about Red? She won't want to live up there like a hermit.'

The valley! We could live in the valley! 'Dad, can I show you something?'

'What?'

'Something up there.'

'I know what's up there. I used to dream about hiding out up there when the station got sold. I searched every valley and gorge. It's just not possible. We can't make a living.'

Silence.

'Can we just go for a drive? See where the rest of the mob went while this mob settle.'

The mares are walking up the laneway toward Roman, caught.

'If we could get the rest of the mob . . . ' Shane goes on.

'All right. All right.' Dad turns around and starts to drive the bull-catcher through the open grassland, leaning out the side, following the horses' tracks.

20

———

Dad and Shane follow the remains of the herd to the lower rocky slopes of the stone country. As they climb higher, they have to leave the bull-catcher and walk. 'We're gonna lose them,' Shane says, hobbling along behind Dad. 'Let's get horses and come back.'

The sun's still high in the sky. There's enough time, so they go back. Dad stops at the saddle shed to get his gear and, leaving Shane at the yards to get Chocolate, drives round to the home paddock to get his stock-horse Snips. 'Meet you at the bottom gate.'

Shane grabs a bridle, lifts a saddle onto his shoulder and walks into the yard. He whistles.

Roman looks up. Chocolate keeps eating, ignoring him.

Should I take Roman? Shane thinks. *He'd know exactly where the mares have gone. Nah, don't be stupid. It's too soon.*

Roman steps forward.

'What do you reckon, mate?' Shane asks him, holding the bridle out to let him sniff it.

Roman nudges the bridle, making the metal tinkle. The smell of leather fills his nostrils and his whole body shivers. Shane puts the saddle on the ground. Talking, keeping eye contact with Roman, he loosens the cheek straps on the bridle to make it bigger.

'You remember this one, hey? You want to see your mares again, don't you?' He holds his breath and lifts the bridle up.

And Roman puts his face into it.

Shane takes another breath and holds the bit against his teeth.

And the big horse opens his mouth and takes the bit.

'Awesome!' Shane pats Roman's face, rubbing him behind the ears. A gentle tug on the reins, and Roman steps forward. Shane holds the saddle blanket up to his face and down his neck, trying to go slowly, not to scare him. He lifts the saddle high on his shoulder, and slowly lowers it onto Roman's back. And then he's up, Roman's body jittering beneath him, ears laid back.

'You right. You right.' Shane moves his weight from side to side. 'You can do it. Look, you're fine.' He leans forward, patting Roman's neck.

'What the bloody hell are you doing?'

Dad.

'He . . .' Then Shane's determined. 'I'm taking Roman. He knows where the mares are.'

'You'll lose him.'

'He's right. Look at him. He's quiet. Anyway, he knows the country. And they trust him.'

'Lose him and we've lost everything.'

'We won't lose him. I promise. Let's go.'

·   ·   ·

Back at the house Mum, Red and Lofty are out on the veranda drinking tea. They see Shane and Dad. Shane's on Roman, taking him out.

Red smiles, *God, that Shane's good with animals,* and she gets up, wanting to sing out to him, to say, *You're the best! But they're going out into the bottom paddock! That's a bit dangerous on a first ride. What happens if Roman throws Shane? That's stupid.* She starts to yell out to them, to tell them to stop, but then she realises that Shane's going up the valley. He's going to show his dad the valley.

She looks at Lofty, sucks her breath in softly to make a quiet whistle to get his attention, and points with her lips.

Lofty looks up, *Whatkind?*, lifting his eyebrows.

Red points. 'They going to that valley,' she whispers.

Lofty looks at her, questioning.

'That valley, secret one.' She points up to the stone country with her chin.

'What?' Mum asks.

Lofty closes his eyes. 'We got to stop them,' he says to Mum, and runs.

Lofty and Red jump in the ute and drive flat out round past Rochter's Pass. Lofty jumps out and starts jogging straight up the hill.

'Not this way. It's around there,' Red yells to him.

Lofty stops and looks at her, shocked. *You question me?*

She drops her eyes and follows.

Roman and Snips pick their way between the rocks. Shane gives Roman his head and he walks quickly, deliberately. He knows exactly where he's going. But it's the wrong way. *The valley was up in there, between those outcrops.* Shane tries to pull him up.

'What?' Dad asks.

'Up in there. There's this valley.'

'Give him his head. We're looking for the mares.'

And so instead of heading toward the valley they pick their way up the back of the steep ranges into country that neither Shane nor Dad has ever seen before, the horses' bodies lifting, jerking, to get up over the rocks.

Roman is sure-footed, walking a path he knows. Snips is clumsy. His hoofs slip and trip.

Higher and higher they go. Gum trees curve around the shapes of the rocks, contorted. Their bark is bone-white, black where fires have licked at their dryness. They look like tortured bodies. Burned skeletons of enemy soldiers. Eerie.

It's so steep that Dad has to get off Snips and walk beside him. Shane knows he won't be able to walk far with his sore leg so he stands in the stirrups, trying to make himself lighter.

They walk and walk, getting deeper and deeper into the hills. 'Get lost that easy in here,' Dad says.

Roman's calm, pushing forward. 'Roman knows where he's going.'

'Looks like we're heading back toward Dead Man's Peak. Could end up stuck out here all night.' Dad says, looking up at the shape of the rocky outcrops around them, trying to recognise something. 'Nah. Sun's still high in the sky,' he relents. 'It's no more than three o'clock. At least four hours of sunlight left. Even if we do get lost, we should be able to find our way back before dark.'

'Look – mare's tracks,' Shane says, pointing to a skid down one of the rocks into the sand.

Dad touches the soil with his finger. 'That's Snips. We're going around in circles.'

'But . . .' Roman's walking so deliberately. 'You sure?'

Dad lifts his eyebrows. *Who doesn't know their own horse's prints?*

'Can we just go just a bit farther?'

Dad looks doubtful, but they continue on. The only sound is the clink of horses' hoofs echoing back to them from the stone.

Suddenly Roman stops and calls.

There's an answer. But where'd it come from?

'Hold him good,' Dad whispers.

Shane shortens the reins and tightens his grip on the saddle. Roman calls again and starts walking quickly. Dad gets back up on Snips and they trot around a tall pillar of stone, through a small passage and into a narrow gorge. The walls are at least forty metres tall, so tall the sun only shines directly into the gorge at midday. Now it's in dark shadow.

'Where is this place? Shane asks. 'Never heard of a gorge up here before.' They pick their way around boulders and large slabs of rock to the creek's edge. The water's crystal clear and rushing. 'Must be spring fed,' Dad says. 'Looks like good water for this time of year.'

They follow a narrow little path along the edge of the creek, pandanus brushing against them, spiking their arms. The path gets narrower and narrower, so they have to duck under branches. They walk and walk and walk. Every now and then Roman calls. Shane looks up into the surrounding landscape for an answer.

But there's nothing.

High in the sky the crested hawk soars, black against the clear blueness, floating on the hot air rising out of the gorge. It watches the horsemen far below, picking their way along the track like an ants at the bottom of a deep chasm.

21

Lofty leaps from rock to rock, arms out, taking wide steps, each bare foot landing solid. His boots, hat and shirt are left far behind, wrapped in a bundle in a tree. Red follows him. He's strong and agile, like a young man: his greyness, his thin old man's body are gone. Now he's moving so fast she has to run to keep up with him. He climbs straight up the hill, his long fingers gripping crevices in the rock.

'Grandad, I can't reach.'

He leans down and takes her hand, his grip so strong that she tries to look into his eyes to see if he really is Lofty, her old grandfather. But he turns away before she can see his face properly. 'Quick,' he says, and continues up the wall of stone.

In the gorge, Shane looks over his shoulder. Dad and Snips are way behind. He can't even see them. And Snips is supposed to be the best stock-horse in the camp! Shane smiles. *He's useless compared to Roman.* 'You're amazing,' he says to Roman. 'And you're mine.' He hugs the horse's neck.

'Really mine. You came to me in the yard, hey?' He remembers how Roman came up to him in the round yard, wanting to please, putting his head in the bridle. 'I reckon I could train you to do anything.'

They're moving through a narrow tunnel of trees. Shane leans forward. His leg is aching. So, next time there's an open space, he lies back along Roman's back, lifting his leg up to rest on the pommel. *That's better.* He relaxes, his head on Roman's rump. 'Tell us when we get there, mate.' He gammon goes to sleep, pulling his hat across his face to block out the sun and putting his arms behind his head.

Roman ignores him. Looking ahead, ears forward, not listening to Shane's voice, he walks quickly along the track.

They're on top of the world, Lofty and Red, standing on massive red stone blocks. The heat bouncing up from them burns Red's face. Blue sky around them. Lofty heads for a deep crevice in the rock, a narrow gorge, only ten metres wide but at least forty metres deep. A crested hawk swoops over his shoulder, surfing the warm wind currents, his head always turning back to watch.

Lofty starts to talk in Language. *To the bird*?

Red looks down. Far below there's a movement. A horse and rider! Her eyes widen. 'Shane! There's Shane!' she yells, pointing down the gorge.

Sit down. Lofty tells her with a curve of his hand. She sits, then he moves back from the edge to sit himself, his legs folded beneath him, his head up, chest out, the long scars along his arms quivering.

'But Grandad, it's Shane.'

'Move back further and sit down,' he yells to her in

Language. 'Sit down and stay still. This is a very dangerous time.'

Lofty's face is so serious that Red starts to obey him straight away, but before she can move a shimmer ripples through the earth. She stops. Her knees feel like jelly. The ground's shaking! Rumbling! It's an earthquake!

'Shane!' she yells. She crawls back to the edge, screaming, 'Shane! It's an earthquake! Run!'

Crack! A split opens up in the rock underneath her. She jumps to one side. 'Grandad!'

Lofty's just sitting there, singing.

'Grandad!' she screams. 'Shane's down there! He's gonna be killed!'

The song comes louder and louder, heavy in the air, solid.

Rumble! Crack! The earth jerks away from her.

'Grandad, run! We've got to . . .' She runs to Lofty, collapsing beside him, holding on to the earth. Safe. It's just the edge moving. She looks up and yes, the rocks on the edge are falling away. 'No!' She imagines the rocks smashing down into the gorge, bouncing off the wall, raining down on Shane, knocking him off the horse. Crushing him. Falling, falling, hundreds of rocks piling on top of him. Roman, just his head sticking out of the mass of broken rock, screaming in pain. 'No!' She covers her face with her hands. 'Shane!'

Lofty sings, and the song spreads around her, mingling with the rumble of the earth, lifting, soothing.

If Shane had been paying attention he might have seen the trees sway, heard the earth grumble. But with his head on Roman's rump, the clack of hoofs in his ears and his mind full of pride, he hears nothing.

Until . . . *Whack!* Something hits him full in the guts, knocking the breath out of him. He sits up, loses his balance, and falls off Roman's back. He tries to get up, winded, can't breathe. Roman's trotting away! No! He jumps up and down, sucking air into his lungs, trying to whistle to chase the horse. 'Roman! Pull up!'

Rocks are falling around him. *What's going on?* The gorge walls are crumbling, huge pieces of rock are smashing to earth, into the creek, splashing water up into the air. The ground's moving! Earthquake! He runs as fast as he can, following Roman down the gorge, dodging rocks, hands over his head, his bruised leg aching.

There's a corner. A dead end!

'No!' he screams, looking up around him at the collapsing walls. *But Roman must have come through here! Where'd he go?*

Then he sees it. Two big boulders stop the narrow gorge. But they don't meet. Between them the creek bubbles and sparkles over rocks. Shane jumps into the creek, slipping on moss. Crouching right down, he crawls through the gap between the boulders.

Red?

Red's leaning against the rock.

'Red!' He runs to her, grabs her.

'Shane!' Her voice is muffled in his shirt.

He pulls her face away. 'Where'dja come from?'

'I don't know. I was with Grandad, then here. I thought you was dead.'

'*I* thought I was dead. There was rocks coming at me from everywhere.'

Silence. They realise they're hanging on to each other and let go. *Shame job.* Everything's calm. There's no rocks on the ground around them. It's as if nothing happened at all.

But, I remember Lofty singing. Red thinks *The rocks were breaking apart beneath me?*

Where's the gorge? Shane thinks. *The walls were collapsing, raining down. Where's Roman? Where's Dad?*

'Dad!'

Shane runs back to the boulders. The gap is blocked. Rocks spill out on the ground in front of it. He grabs for rocks, starts throwing them behind him.

'What ya doing?'

'Dad was following me. He's in there.' Tears run down Shane's face. He's tossing rocks out between his legs like a dog digging. His father is buried. Dead.

'Shane. Stop. I didn't see him. He wasn't there.'

Shane's grabbing and throwing, grabbing and throwing, but as soon as he makes a space more rocks fall into it.

'Shane, stop! Me and Lofty were up there.' She points to the cliff. 'It was just you on Roman. Your dad wasn't in the gorge.'

He hears her and slows down, his face brown with dust.

'You were the only movement. True story.'

Shane turns his face away, embarrassed, wiping the sweat and tears from his cheeks.

They look around. Silence. No rocks. No dust. The sun is going down orange over the hills. The last rays of light shine golden on the top of the cliffs and reflect back into the valley. *The valley?*

'Red?'

She's walking down the path.

'Red, don't! This is that valley!' Shane runs and grabs her arm. 'Look. It's exactly the same as it was that day.'

'It can't be. It can't look the same if we came in from a

totally different side. We came right around the back of Dead Man's Peak. The track was . . . We didn't . . .'

But it is! There's the thick forest of trees, the leaf litter. The ironwood trees, their bright, wet season leaves sparkling in the sun. And over there on the left-hand side a line of the kind of dark green vegetation that defines a spring-fed creek.

Red is thirsty. So thirsty. Her body tries to resist, her brain tries to find the memory of danger, but it's too vague. She can't fight the desperate need to drink. Cool water fills her mind.

Shane holds her, but his grip is weak. 'I need a drink,' he says, and they walk together, disappearing down through the trees.

And with a moan, rocks and earth settle into the gap behind them, closing it up completely.

22

'Shane!' Dad yells.

Shane, Shane, Shaaane, the stone around him answers.

'You little bugger! Stop stuffing around!'

Ound ound ound, the stone whispers.

There's no movement anywhere. Just tall walls of red stone. Shane has vanished.

Snips is dragging his feet, exhausted. He stops, head down. Dad urges him forward, but he won't move. Somewhere in the distance rocks are falling, *clunk, clunk,* bouncing down a hillside. And behind that, somewhere, there's a sound. A strange song oozing out of the air. It's a Bunuba song, coming from the cliffs. The song floats, soaking up the noise, slowing the rocks' fall, dulling the impact as they hit the ground.

Dad's tired, so tired. The sun has gone behind the hills. Around him the rocks are purple and cool in the shade. 'Just rest a bit, old fella,' he tells Snips, and he leans against a boab tree, Snips' reins looped through his arm. 'Just a minute, then we've got to find him. Gotta find Shane.'

His body relaxes, the song soothing him into sleep. He dreams. There is a tall red tower. Tiny high holes cut into the mud. A prison. Sitting up in one of the windows is a man, a black man, an old ceremony man, his hair matted at the back of his head, his back curved into the window shape, legs tucked into his chest. He looks out, far out into the distance, singing. Looking and singing for his country.

You can see the song float out into the air, moving across the land like a shimmer of heat; through the trees, above the rivers, over floodplains, across the open woodland and up into the stone country. It travels all the thousands of kilometres from Rottnest Island prison to the Kimberley. To the land coming empty now, shaking with loss. Under the surface the rock is bubbling with anger. Wallabies stop, their ears twitching, black men on horseback stand and listen. Then they take up the song, calling it out. And it moves through the country like a stroking hand, soothing, calming, settling the great turmoil into silence. Until the only sound is the cattle eating spinifex seeds and the clack of hoofs against rock echoing through the gorges and caves.

'Old man.' Someone touches Dad's shoulder.

'Lofty?' The dream disappears. It's nearly dark. 'Shane? Where's Shane?'

'He's right.'

'Come on.' Dad stands up. 'We gotta find him. He's on Roman.'

'They're all right,' Lofty says.

'Where's Red?'

Lofty points to the hills with his lips. *Why is he so calm?*

'Come on!' Dad yells. 'Get bikes and torches and come

back before . . .' He calls Snips and steps up into the saddle. 'That bloody horse's thrown him. Stupid. Stupid. Why'd I let him take it?'

Lofty swings up behind him and Snips trots with his sure-footed, loose gait over the rocks and logs, through the narrow passages, and down the hillside. Then, as fast as they dare in the darkness, they canter back on Snips to the homestead.

Dad jumps down and runs straight into Shane's room to get some dirty clothes, something that's been worn, that will have Shane's scent on it so the dogs can follow his tracks.

Lofty follows. He wants to say, *Shane's alive, don't worry. Red couldn't have gone to him if he was dead. They'll be all right. We do need to get them before the country swallows them. But they are safe. They are alive.*

But he notices a shelf along the wall. A shelf of weapons. Bunuba weapons, old ones, from olden time, kept, collected. Trophies? Like buffalo horns? Trophies of the war. *Of the policemen and the settlers hunting my people.*

There's a small pile of bullet heads. He picks them up, feels the weight of them in his palm. He turns to Dad. 'Whatkind?'

Dad takes one out of Lofty's palm. 'Winchester forty-four,' he says. 'That's what the coppers used in the early days.'

Lofty's staring at him, saying, *I know.*

'They're whole. No dents. Like they've been dug out of something soft.' Dad looks up and meets Lofty's eyes, dark pools of anger.

Dad's heart sinks. *A body. They've been taken out of a body. Hell Shane, where did you get these?*

Lofty is sitting on the bed, his fist closed tight over the bullet heads. Dad sits beside him in silence, thinking, waiting.

'I dreamed about one old man, ceremony man,' he says at last. 'Up there when I sat down, I dreamed they took him away to jail and he sent his song all the way home to the country, to make it quiet.'

Silence.

'I heard that same song today. For real. When Shane disappeared. That was you?'

Lofty says nothing. He can feel Dad's eyes on him. 'I thought all that stuff was finished.'

Silence.

'Lofty, you got to tell me what's going on.'

Lofty looks at him.

'Whatever it is, we have to fight this together.'

'What's wrong?' Mum's at the door.

Silence.

'Where are the kids?' Then, seeing their faces, 'Lofty?' Her face is white, eyes wide.

'They're all right. We just got separated,' Dad says, his voice loud. 'We're going back up now to get them.'

'Well, what are you waiting for?' She rushes out the door to grab the torches and first aid kit.

Lofty drags himself up off the bed, exhausted.

Dad goes outside. He whistles to the dogs and they jump in the back of the bull-catcher. Lofty walks to the bull-catcher, looks Dad right in the eye and steps into the driver's seat.

For the first time in his adult life Dad slips into the passenger seat. As the bull-catcher takes off he feels loose, unattached, without the steering wheel to hold on to. He rolls a smoke in the dark to do something with his hands. They drive along slowly, the hand-held spotlights scanning the paddocks and open country on either side of the track.

23

———

Shane and Red walk down the track to the flat, and there is the creek, skipping over rocks and logs, sparkling gold and silver in the evening sun.

They run to it, kneel down to suck the coolness of water into themselves. Sucking it up in big gulps, till their throats sting with a lump and their stomachs are bloated. But still they're thirsty, so they soak their hands and feet in the creek, splash water on their faces with cupped hands. And finally they climb in and lie among the orange root-tips and soak the water up through their pores, letting it fill them with moisture as if they are trees. Soaking. Until, plump and ripe, they relax and look around.

A dragonfly, purple and red, lands on a long blade of grass, and the grass bends slowly into the water to let it drink. Above the creek, strung between the trees, is a huge golden orb spider's web, the strands thick as cotton. In the middle is the spider, big as a hand, orange and black with iridescent knee pads, huge ball eyes watching. An azure kingfisher drops into the water with a flash of purple. Something scurries in the grass. A bandicoot? A water rat?

No – much bigger – slithering on the ground like a big snake or goanna. Shane and Red move closer together and stand up to see. It stops. They stare at the grass till their eyes go unfocused but can't see anything.

'Probably a blue-tongue,' Shane says.

'Bit big for a blue-tongue.'

The sun disappears behind the cliffs, but the radiance of it reflects back off the clouds making the world lighter not darker; giving the land more depth, so that it looks sculptured. The stone walls seem so close you could touch them.

They struggle to climb out of the water. Their saturated clothes weigh them down. A cool breeze runs across the tops of the grasses, bending the seed heads, chilling their wet clothes, turning Red's lips purple and Shane's blue. They start to shiver.

'We need a fire.'

'No matches.'

'Flint? What sort of stone? Rub two sticks together?' Red's teeth are chattering.

They move closer. 'Probably shouldn't light a fire,' Shane says. He doesn't say, *We don't know what sort of creatures a fire would attract in this ancient place, cut off from the rest of the world.* But that's what he's thinking.

'Make a hide.' They break leafy branches and make a bed on the ground beneath a pandanus clump. 'We'll be safe here. Be able to hear a mouse move in them pandanus leaves.'

They climb into the bed and cover themselves with leaf litter. Mozzies start to whine around their ears and bite them through their wet clothes. They snuggle down farther into the leaves, conscious of being so close together, trying not to touch.

The first star shines bright between the trees.

'Make a wish.'

Roman. Please make Roman safe . . . No, Dad. Please make sure Dad is okay.

Grandad. Please make Grandad safe.

They lie side by side, watching the stars come into focus as the darkness deepens. Shane tries to think about what happened. How did they end up here in the valley again, cut off, isolated? What should they do? But he can't worry. It feels so right to be here, so close together, alone.

Red rolls over on her side and moves towards him, to feel his warmth against her back.

The moon is up, spreading its soft light through the trees, shining on the curve of Red's cheek, the brightness of her hair.

Shane puts his arm around her and moves closer, feeling the tickle of her hair on his nose.

Red snuggles back into him. 'Don't get any ideas, Shane,' she teases.

Shane's face tingles like it's been slapped. He rolls away from her. 'As if!' he says, closing his eyes tight with shame.

But he can't stay wild. He can still remember the warmth of her skin against his arm, his chest. He imagines her smile, how it crinkles up her eyes; her brave, serious face, breaking into laughter. I don't care if we never get out, he thinks. I don't care if we have to live here in the valley for ever. There's plenty of tucker. We'll get married. In his mind he sees them getting married by the creek, Red with purple and yellow wildflowers in her hair.

Red folds her arms around herself, hurt, angry. *I hate him,* she thinks, staring into the night. *As if. I was just joking! Why's everything so serious with you, Shane?* She lies still, bitterness snarling her mouth. She's freezing, freezing cold, but she stays right away from Shane's warmth.

'Sleep now, baby child,' she sings in her mother's language in her mind. 'Breathe your mother's breath.' It's the song her mother always sang to her to put her to sleep when she was little. And then she is asleep, and dreaming.

Her mother is walking into the stockyards. She's going up to the stock-horses, a rough myall looking mob of brumbies, their heads down, uninterested, sullen. Red's up on Lofty's shoulders, watching, as she did so often as a child.

Her mother laughs and sings to them in her language, 'You are brave, strong, beautiful creatures.'

The horses lift their heads.

'You are power, rippling muscle, light and sure of foot. With your massive hearts you can gallop faster than the wind.'

Their dull eyes brighten and they come forward to meet her, pushing their heads under her arms.

Red wakes up. Stars shine softly in the night sky. Why has she never remembered that scene before? The song is still there in her mind. 'Brave, strong, beautiful creatures,' she sings. 'Power, rippling muscle, sure feet, gallop with the wind.' She hasn't heard her mother's and grandmother's language for years, but the words come back.

Shane rolls over toward her in his sleep, his breathing slow and heavy in her ear.

So Mum really did have the words to talk with horses, Red thinks. Grandad's story is true. Them myall old brumbies came to her. They wanted to please her. She closes her eyes and relaxes her back against Shane, playing the song over in her mind: 'Brave, strong, beautiful creatures. Power, rippling muscle, sure feet, gallop in the wind.'

Rustle. There's a noise in the grass. Red opens her eyes. The moon is dropping behind the valley wall. She has been asleep for hours.

Something is moving through the grass. Shane's eyes spring open; his body stiffens. Red slips her hand down to grabs his hand, saying, *I'm awake.*

There is definitely something there. It's not in the pandanus leaves yet, but . . . *Shuffle. Snort. Shiver.* It's a huge animal. Really close.

They turn their heads slow and steady so they can see. There it is. A huge dark shape. Black against the sky. Great lumps along its back, bumpy points, moving like . . . a massive caterpillar?

Crunch! Snort! Shiver!

They are absolutely still. Then there's a tinkle. Like metal. Like . . .

Their eyes hurt, trying to focus. *Snort! Shiver! Rattle!* It's the horses! The shiver of skin moving over bone. And metal, a bridle. It's Roman!

Shane eases himself up to see. Yes! It's the horses. You can see their individual shapes now. Not just a mass of flesh. Hard to see how they looked like a . . . what? A monster caterpillar? He smiles.

They're moving away. Red grabs Shane's arm and pulls it to say, *Let's follow. If there's a way out, the horse will know it.*

They stand up, leaves rustling around them. The horses stop, dead still, ears forward, searching the night for danger.

Shane crosses his fingers and legs for luck and whistles softly to Roman.

Silence.

He whistles louder. Roman answers.

Red wraps her hand around Shane's crossed-over fingers to give them strength, and Shane whistles again.

Roman steps forward.

'Hey, big bloke,' Shane says softly.

Roman comes closer, whinnying. And then his soft nose nudges Shane, nearly knocking him off his crossed-over-for-luck legs.

The big brood mare calls out to Roman, warning him. Shane reaches his hand out for the reins, but Roman lifts his head, turning, moving away. Shane calls again, but Roman ignores him. He keeps walking until he is back with the herd.

Gotta stop him, but if we move, they'll bolt. We'll never be able to follow them in the dark.

Then Red steps forward, talking – no – *singing* in Language. Shane reaches out to grab her arm, to tell her to stop, not to scare the horses, but she shakes him off. 'Come, you brave, strong, beautiful horses,' she sings, her voice barely above a whisper.

The horses lift their heads, concentrating, trying to hear. Roman is in front, dead still, listening.

'Roman, you are power, rippling muscle.' Red's voice is louder now in the still night air. She can't find all the words so she lets the thoughts flow, mixing Lofty's language, Kriol, English and her mother's language.

Shane holds his breath. The mares stomp their legs, snorting the human smell out of their nostrils. They hold their heads high and alert, ready to bolt.

The big brood mare walks up to Roman, murmuring her fear to him.

'Mother,' Red tells her, 'your feet are sure, your heart huge.'

Silence.

'You licked my mother's birth blood to give her breath. We are connected, you and I.'

The big mare tosses her head up and down, murmuring.

'You are powerful, intelligent, you know this land. Take us with you.'

And the mare steps forward. Right up to Red. Touching her outstretched hand. Breathing her in.

Shane moves slowly around Red and walks up to Roman. 'Hey, big man. Big horse.'

Roman stands. Shane leans forward, takes the reins, and steps up into the saddle before Roman can move. 'Here,' he says, reaching out his hand to Red to swing her up behind him.

But Red rubs her hand down the mare's neck, to her shoulder. The mare leans into her, accepting. And Red grabs a handful of mane and swings up onto her back.

The horses walk out of the greyness of the open country and into the dimness beneath the trees, heads down, checking the dark earth for safe passage. Shane and Red can't see anything, but they hear the horses' hoofs first crunching on grass, then padding on soft sand and finally clanking and slipping on rock as they move out of the valley, down, down, out of the stone country to the lower slopes of rock and gravel. Now the sky is clear above them, stars sparkling behind the silhouettes of leaf and twig. And in no time, they're out in the open country, heading for the floodplain. Safe.

138

24

Dad and Lofty are in the front of the bull-catcher, Lofty driving. Mum's in the back, screaming out into the night, 'Shane! Red!'. The dogs rush around searching for a scent, finding nothing.

'This is definitely the way we came,' Dad says.

Lofty whistles up the dogs and turns the bull-catcher around, heading up toward the jump-up.

Dad looks at him. He wants to argue, to say, *We didn't go that way*. But Lofty's so serious, so completely in charge, Dad doesn't know how to talk to him.

One of the dogs barks, grabbing the scent, and runs with it, nose down, into the bush.

'Yes!' Mum and Dad jump out of the bull-catcher holding the spotlights, and run with the dogs.

The dogs stop.

'Come on, what's the matter?'

They're running around in circles. They've lost the scent. Mum and Dad run back to the bull-catcher and Lofty drives on.

The spotlights shine through the bush, lighting up gnarled thin trunks, shrubs and massive blocks of stone. Outside the beams of light there is darkness, pitch black darkness.

They try another track.

The dogs pick up a scent again and run off, but as soon as they get among the stones, they lose it. It happens time and time again until most of the night's gone and the moon's hanging near the horizon.

Dad is losing heart. Something is wrong, badly wrong. That bloody horse has thrown Shane. He's lying dead some-where. Red's lost. Or they've both been thrown. Wouldn't put it past them two to try doubling on that mongrel horse.

Light! Spotlights arcing through the bush. *Voices.* 'Shane! Red!' Mum's voice is urgent.

The light spins around and smacks into their eyes, blinding.

Shane grabs Roman's reins. 'Stand up. It's okay.' He closes his eyes. Roman jerks to a stop, dancing, ready to run.

'Keep the light on them,' Lofty calls, wanting to keep the horses blinded so they can't bolt.

'Get in behind!' Dad yells, and the dogs dive into the back of the bull-catcher, whining, excited.

The horses neigh quietly to each other but stand still. They can't see.

'Shane?' Dad's voice calls into the darkness.

'Yeah. We're here. We're all right. Got Roman and the mares.'

'Red?' Lofty calls.

'Yes, Grandfather. I'm here. I see you,' she says in

Language. 'They came to us, Grandfather. They gave themselves to us.'

'Dad, this is our breeding stock. We're gonna be all right,' Shane says.

Dad wants to say, *Forget the horses. I don't care about anything except you. Just get in the car where I know you're safe.* But instead he says, 'We'll follow you up as soon as you get down to the floodplain.'

'Thanks Dad.'

One by one they lower the spotlights. Easy and slow. Not making a sound. They stay absolutely still so they don't spook the horses.

'Stand up. You right.'

It takes a minute before the horses can see again. Then Shane and Red urge Roman and the big mare through the open country and out onto the floodplain, the herd following them close behind.

By and by with the bull-catcher pushing them from behind, the horses go straight up beside the hessian-fence, along the laneway and into the spelling yard.

The sky is already starting to lighten in the east before the horses are safe in behind the high wire, watered and fed.

'Cuppa?' Lofty asks.

Shane and Red look round, shocked. Mum and Dad don't have cuppas at Lofty's place. They drink around the stockyard fire. They take a thermos down to the yards when they start work early. But mostly if they want to talk, they always go up to the big house.

Mum wraps her arms around Red and Shane. 'Yeah. Come on.'

Everyone is quiet while Lofty kicks the fire into life and puts the billy on to boil. But once they're sitting around on blankets and upturned tins, drinking sweet black tea, Shane and Red can't stop talking. 'You was right behind me,' Shane tells Dad. 'Next minute there's rocks falling and I'm running for my life.'

'It was the same valley,' Red interrupts.

'Same as what?'

So they have to tell about the first time. About how they pretended to be doing the essay. How their footprints disappeared.

They look at Lofty. 'How did you know?'

Lofty looks at them, his eyebrows lifted to say, *What do you think. Of course I knew. I know everything.*

Then they're off again, interrupting each other. 'Gammon. You goonahed yourself too!' And Shane tells about Red. How she started to sing this song in Language and the horses understood what she was saying. How the big mare came to her.

'Just like your mother, May. She could quieten any old myall horse,' Dad says, impressed.

Lofty smiles at Red. 'You subbie, my girl?' he asks, his voice quiet.

Red puts her head down, nods, embarrassed. 'My mother came to me in a dream and taught me that song,' she says in Language.

Lofty sits back in his chair and looks at Red and Shane sitting together on a blanket, talking like one person. *They're growing up now.* His blood rushes with worry. Red must have all the knowledge, so she can make the right decisions. So she can go to boarding school and university but still come back to this country. Her country. Because it is her country. It opened itself up to her – it has claimed her now.

Lofty touches the bullet heads in his pocket. Then he sits up tall in his chair. 'I've been walking this country long time,' he says. 'Eighty years more or less.' He looks at Dad. 'Your father and grandfather too. And it never showed itself to us, that secret place, hey?' He asks Dad to confirm what he's saying.

Dad nods.

'That place has given itself to these young people. We must give them everything, all the stories of our history. We have to make it safe for them.'

Silence.

Then Lofty starts the story the way he's started it many times before. 'Jandamarra, he is a police tracker. He can find anyone.'

Red smiles, relaxing, letting the familiar words wash over her.

Only this time Lofty doesn't stop when Jandamarra is victorious in the hills. He finishes the story – the whole story. 'For years they hunt him,' he says. 'For years Jandamarra holds the cattle back from his land. No one can kill him. He's a clever man, a businessman. They shoot him plenty times but he doesn't die.'

Everyone sits mesmerised.

'But now everyone is finished, his wife, his mother, all his family. Jandamarra is the only one left.'

A long silence.

'And now the police find a clever man, Minko Mick from Roebourne. He can fight Jandamarra. He has the spiritual powers of Jalnggangurru. 'Come help us', they say.

'I can kill Jandamarra,' Minko Mick says. 'I can kill any kind of clever man.'

'Minko Mick comes walking. He doesn't come fast. He sleeps there listening to the country all the way. One day. Three days. One week, he walks.'

Silence.

'Now Minko Mick, the station people and all the policemen hunt Jandamarra. They shoot him many times.'

Red interrupts, 'But Minko was Aboriginal. Why would he—'

Lofty lifts his finger to say, *Wait.*

'Now it's early morning. Jandamarra is nearly finished. He has lost too much blood. He takes himself to the edge of that cliff in Windjana Gorge. He yells out to Minko Mick. 'Come out in the open and fight', he says.

'Minko Mick is hiding there behind that boab tree.

'Jandamarra shoots at him.

'Minko Mick waits. He sneaks around the side. Minko Mick shoots. He hits Jandamarra in the hand.

'Jandamarra falls, all that way, right from the top he falls, smashing on the rock below. Finished.'

'My great-grandfather, was he there?' Shane says.

Lofty holds up his finger to say, *Be quiet.* Then he pulls the bullet heads from his pocket.

How'd he get them? He's been in my room!

Lofty looks into Shane's eyes and then Red's to make sure they're listening. 'That policeman cuts off Jandamarra's head. To prove. They want to make a big celebration. So, they cut off Jandamarra's head and send that head to Perth, like a trophy. The big government man lined the head up on a shelf in the museum.' Lofty looks directly at Shane. 'They put that head there for a collection.'

Shane lowers his eyes.

'All the people come now to the museum,' Lofty says. 'They gave that government money to stare at Jandamarra's head.'

Silence.

Lofty pauses to let the words settle over his audience. 'The police are gone now. The people go back. They find Jandamarra's body there – no head. They wrap it in paperbark, put it there in a cave. When that body flesh is gone, just bullet heads and bones left, they put those bones in the sacred cliff. They tried to make a proper burial for him but no skull.'

They sit in silence around the fire, their faces changing in shadow and light. They have no words to talk about this. It's a fresh wound, too raw for picking.

Was my great-grandfather there? Shane's thinking. Did he help to hunt the people – help to kill Jandamarra?

He feels sick in the guts.

Red's mind is racing. *Minko Mick? How could an Aboriginal person do that? Why didn't Jandamarra fight the policemen? What about Shane's great-grandfather? I wonder if he was there? She looks at Shane.*

He's got his head down.

She tries to count back. How long has his family been here? 'When did Jandamarra die?' she asks Lofty in Language.

Dad looks up. *It was 1897,* he wants to say. *It's in that Jandamarra book – 1897. That's three years before my grandfather came, so we weren't involved in these killings.* But if he says that, it will sound like he's just trying to get out of it – denying responsibility – making out like his family didn't do anything wrong. So he says nothing.

'Long. Long time ago,' Lofty answers her.

That's no good, Red thinks. *I want dates. I want to know if they were involved. If Shane's great-grandfather was there. What did his mum say today" That the old man came up in 1900. That's right. Because the first entry in the station book was Doris. What did it say? Doris 1902. Red hair. ½ C. What's ½ C? Half-caste! That's what they used to call people who had a malngarri father.*

Her gut drops. She breathes deep and looks up at Lofty. 'Grandfather, who was Doris's father? Was he malngarri?' she asks in Language.

Lofty looks at Dad. Their eyes hold for a minute. Then, when Dad looks away, Lofty says, 'You wait.' He points to the dawn rising. 'We finished with talking for now. We'll come together again, all of us, and we will have all the stories.'

The sun peeks orange over the hills. 'Gawarra rarra imi,' Dad says out loud, speaking the Language words for sunrise. His voice surprises him. He hasn't spoken Language for years. Why? He struggles, searching in his mind for a reason. It's just not part of his life anymore. Is it arrogance? Only seeing the land in terms of profit? *When was the last time you went fishing?* he asks himself. *Hunting? Walking? Seeing? Being in the country.* He looks up at the blue range in the distance behind the homestead. 'Woonamn. Remember we camped up in there one time?' he says to Lofty in Language. 'Three weeks. Only thing we took was tea, flour and sugar. You are a good hunter, old man.'

Lofty smiles, acknowledging the compliment. 'You subbie too,' he says. 'You forgot. But you can catch it again.'

· · ·

As Mum, Dad and Shane walk back to the big house, the land surrounds them. The stone country is purple in the early morning light, the floodplain white with mist. *People were murdered for this land. Does that make us murderers? Thieves?* The paddocks around them sparkle with dew; the fences and laneways, yards and buildings catch the golden light.

Dad thinks, *Stolen? It doesn't feel stolen. It feels like mine. The station my family carved from a wilderness.*

But it wasn't wilderness. It was someone's home.

Justifications and accusations flit like tiny bats through their minds. But the truth hangs around them in the moist air, grating against the tin plates as they feed the dogs; clunking with the cans as they drop, one on top of the other, in the rubbish bin; whispering in the sound of the dogs as they gulp, gulp their food.

And it settles in around Lofty and Red as they pick up the blankets and shake the dust from them, and put the pannikins up on the bench away from the dogs.

For a time their two different histories cut wounds in Red and Shane's hearts, straining their friendship. But then the rawness fades and the stories settle into their minds, acknowledged in the vast sky lit with stars; the towers of stone, the books, oral histories, stories and songs of their people, and in their children, who grow up with all the stories, to live in and worship the stone country.

GLOSSARY

- bull-catcher – a four-wheeled vehicle with no roof or doors
- bullock – a bull that has been castrated
- businessman – a ceremony man who owns all the songs and stories of his land.
- cleanskin – an animal that has never been caught, branded or castrated
- cutting horse – a horse (often a Quarter Horse) used in cattle drafting competitions
- dinnertime – the midday meal time, about twelve noon
- directly – after a while
- donkey trap – a simple portable pole-and-wire yard used to trap donkeys, cattle and horses
- draft – to separate cattle from the herd
- flat – open grassy plain without trees
- gammon – pretend; not real life
- goonah – faeces

- hunt – to chase or drive away, or force into captivity
- Kriol – a language created by Aboriginal people to help them communicate with settlers. The grammar is predominantly Aboriginal while many of the words derive from English. It is a very common language in North Australia.
- malngarri - Europeans, or people who are not Aboriginal
- micky bull – a young wild bull
- milk gut – offal
- muster – the act of rounding up livestock
- myall – not properly trained; not educated; no manners
- Quarter Horse – a horse bred for speed over short distances (originally, a quarter of a mile), and used for roping and drafting cattle
- ringer – a person who works with cattle
- spell – a time to rest and recover
- subbie – understand, have knowledge about
- **Bunuba Language**
- balili – limestone country
- barurra – open grassy plain
- bulumana – bullock
- gawarra rarra imi – the sun coming up
- Jalnggangurru – clever man who has all the songs and stories of the land and is able to communicate with spirits
- wajarri – boab tree
- woonamn – blue range in the distance

ACKNOWLEDGMENTS

Acknowledgments

To my brother Shane for his story; the Bunuba people for permission to use their language and the Jandamarra story; Brent Williamson and my son Shane for suffering hours of 'So do you reckon . . .' and 'What about . . .'; the Kimberley for inspiration; Kate and Greg for the peace of their Kakadu home; Penny Matthews for her insightful editing; Kim Caraher for lifting Red and her mother from the shadows; Rosie Brendan and Dan for their wonderful criticism; my brothers and sons for their love of the land; and my husband Alan for keeping me while I wrote this book.

This writing of this book was assisted by a grant from the Commonwealth Government through the Australia Council, its arts funding and advisory body.

Words from the song 'Buffalo Bill', composed by Sara Storer (ABC Music) are reproduced with permission.

ABOUT THE AUTHOR

Leonie Norrington is an award-winning Australian author. She grew up in remote north Australia in two cultures that were worlds apart. Her education, way of life and spirituality are steeped in the traditions of both the Mayili and Yolngu families who adopted her, and her Irish Catholic heritage.

Leonie worked as a hairdresser, farm hand, fruit picker and nurseryman. It was not until she was in her 30s, after she was married with three children, that she decided to return to school and finish year 12, and then go on to university. There she discovered her talent as a writer; a talent she uses in collaboration with her Mayili and Yolngu families to foster north Australian voices in literature. She is writing a PhD in Creative Arts, under the supervision of Yolngu knowledge holders from North East Arnhem Land.

ALSO BY LEONIE NORRINGTON

The Barrumbi Kids

The Spirit of Barrumbi

Leaving Barrumbi

Croc Bait

Crocodile Jack

Loosing Reuben

Bush Holiday

Brigid Lucy ~~wants~~ NEEDS *a friend*

Brigid Lucy and the Princess Tower

Brigid Lucy wants a Pet

Look See, Look at Me

You and Me: Our Place

The Devil You Know